MEET-CUTE ME UNDER THE MISTLETOE

ID JOHNSON

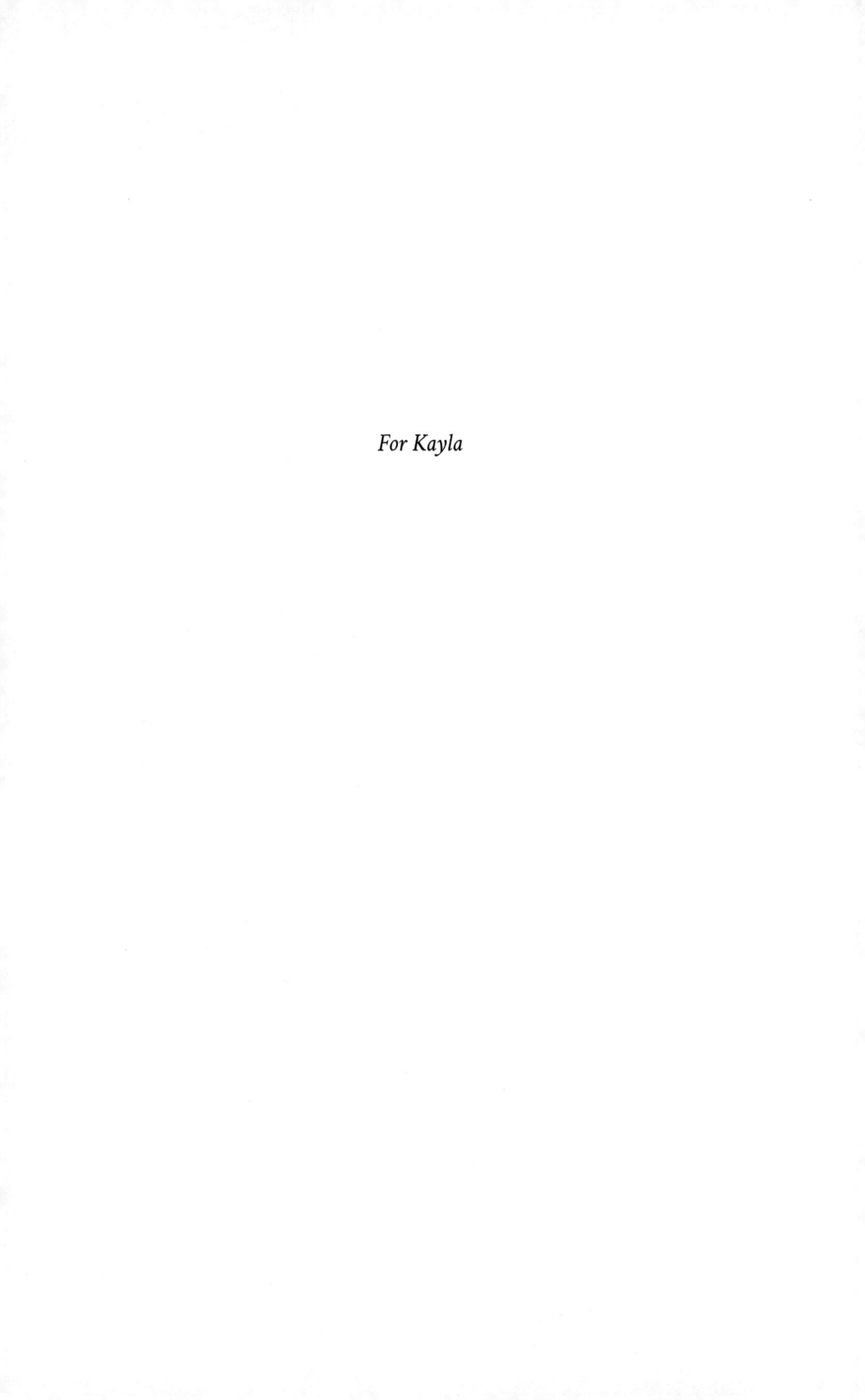

For Kayla

CONTENTS

CHAPTER 1

Holly

I SHOULD HAVE EXPECTED MY PARENTS' bakery to be busy with the official kickoff of Christmas starting this weekend, but the mountains of boxes of Christmas cookies piled on the counter and near the back door were clear evidence that Christmas was in full swing. And I knew it wasn't a minute too soon as I caught a glimpse of the first snow beginning to fall flake by fluffy flake outside the small window in the bakery's back room. I topped one final swirl of baby Jesus' hair on his sugar cookie-baked head. *Perfect,* I thought, but the sound of my mom calling to me from the front of the store brought me out of the zone.

"Holly! You're fixin' to be late if you don't get out of here soon!" she called. It was a sweet, sugar-coated, well-meaning threat. I was my parents' only kid, and while I'd been a regular attendee of the Santa Claus Ball for my whole life, this was the first year I would be attending as a single adult woman. I technically could have participated in the one adult activity–mistletoe kissing–for a few years now, but I had missed out because I hadn't made it home from the dorms in time for my first three years of college. But considering my mom's love for the Santa Claus Ball, you could say she was a little eager to see me off, not to mention the assumed and unsaid reason she was so excited for me to go....

"Are you sure you guys can keep up here?" I asked though I was already lifting the apron over my head. "I can stay a little longer...."

"Holly Lane Garland, you are going to leave this sweet-toothed beast to us, the owners–"

"And Jack!" my father added.

"Yes, yes, and Jack," my mother said. I could imagine the way her eyes rolled around in their sockets as she recalled sweet, freckle-faced Jack, the young man they were training to help manage the bakery as they geared up for retirement. It seemed my father was all for more free time, while my mother was hesitant to lay down her oven mitts and her piping bags. She'd built this place from the ground up–literally–and after they'd married, my dad agreed to help her manage it.

I poked my head around the curtain draped across the doorway leading from the storefront to the back room. I spotted my mom ringing up a new customer while my dad walked toward the front door with his arms full of four boxes of snowman cupcakes. As much as he was ready to relax and spend some leisure time with my mom, he never slowed down. For her sake, he barreled on through, even as the arthritis creeped into his knees, giving him a distinctive hobble.

I imagined him walking out and spotting the silver-white of snow flurrying from the sky and explaining to the customer he was following that his knees had been telling him all morning that snow was due.

"We've only got a couple more hours left before Jack shows up to kickstart the rest of tomorrow's orders," she said after sending her customer away with a smile. She turned to me and leaned back against the register. "I'm telling you, cookie, we'll be fine. We've been doing this longer than you've been alive."

I sighed, glancing back at the full, chaotic kitchen behind me. As fun and exciting as it was to help my mom decorate cookies, especially during the Christmas season, I felt a little overwhelmed by what people expected of them. How had they managed this madness by themselves for so long?

Just then, I felt the distinctive double vibration indicative of a text message for my phone in my back pocket. I patted the little bits of flour dust from my hands before I grabbed it. It was Gretchen. Her text read, "Don't forget that you need to pick up your mask and your dress," and then, "Are you coming here or am I going there?" then, "Maybe your house is better? It's closer." A split second later, she added, "Can I borrow that extra pair of Mary Janes you have?"

I chuckled. Gretchen was my organized mess of a best friend, and she was looking forward to the Santa Claus Ball just as much as I was. I wasn't sure if her boyfriend knew it, but every special occasion for the last two months had sent her into an excited tizzy, anticipating the moment he'd finally pop the question.

I shot back a quick line of messages.

"My house."

"My shoes."

"My dear best friend...."

"Please don't forget to breathe."

When I glanced up from my phone, my mom was smiling softly at me, amused and surely annoyed that I hadn't left yet.

"Mom, c'mon," I said, walking up to her and leaning against the counter next to her. "How many other girls do you know who are willing to put off leaving for a party to spend a few extra minutes with their mother?"

She craned her neck up at me and tucked the loose strand of peppered gray hair behind her ear. She did that slow blink she always made when she was giving in to my or my dad's wishes.

"Okay, then, tell me about the Santa Claus Ball. How are you doing your hair? Are you gonna kiss anyone?" She blinked her eyes expectantly at her last remark.

I'd been fed captivating stories about the Santa Claus Ball since I was a baby. It was where my mother and father met twenty-four years ago, after all. But she'd painted so many beautiful scenes in my mind, magical scenes really, of the silver and gold shining off the

Christmas garland, the tantalizing smell of hot toddy and pie. She had spoken about how the dazzling shine of the multi-color Christmas lights had felt so alluring that she was sure she was in a dream. And when my dad tapped her on the shoulder and asked her to dance, she'd been entranced by the low tenor of his voice and the gentle way he'd led her in the dance. When they took off their Christmas masks and revealed their faces, her breath had caught in her throat because of the young man's bright shining eyes and radiating smile.

My mom never said anything to make me believe that she expected the same thing to happen to me, but I could tell that there was a small smidgen of hope reserved for just that. And it was Christmas, that special time of year my mom went softer than butter in a hot pan for all things love and cheer. She was a sucker for Christmas —she wasn't shy about admitting that their first encounter was directly related to my arguably overly-Christmasy name. And I'd managed to obtain a large part of that character trait, too, but with a more subtle approach.

While I was in awe of my parents' love and marriage, I wasn't so naive to believe every love was like that. I'd had friends of divorced parents, met women and men alike in college who were in tortuous relationships. So I had decided a long time ago–and after I learned that the son of Santa Claus in the Santa Clause movies had grown up and had children of his own by now–that I would take my time. I would focus on school first and worry about love later, one thing at a time.

"Mom, really? You're not going to ask about the foods I'm going to eat or the decorations?" I said, raising an eyebrow.

"What can I say?" she said with a shrug. "I'm up to my elbows in deserts all day every day. I wanna hear about the other sweet stuff."

I couldn't help but chuckle. "You'd think you were the twenty-two-year-old college student and not me."

My dad had just shut the door behind him and wiped his feet on the Christmas present-shaped welcome mat. "Oh, if there's anything that makes this old tree sap up, it's the Santa Claus Ball." He leaned over the counter and kissed my mom on the hair. "Though you'd think meeting me there was enough for her."

This was becoming too much, even for me, so I decided to change the subject. "Gretchen thinks that Joey will propose to her this time."

My mom's and dad's ears both perked up at that.

"Hasn't she been thinking that since the Fourth of July?" my dad muttered.

"Do you think he will?" she asked.

I shrugged. "I guess you never know."

A short, quiet moment passed as each of us thought about it. "It would be quite sweet if he did," my mom said.

"But I hope she doesn't get her hopes up too high," my dad added.

I nodded in agreement. I was all for Joey and Gretchen getting hitched, but this occasion felt a little too on the nose for them.

"Are any of your college friends coming?" my mother asked after a moment.

I shook my head. "Nah, they're too far away. Maybe they'll come up for one of the bigger events though."

"That's a shame," my dad said, coming around the counter and patting me on the shoulder. "It's been a few months since you've seen them, right?"

It was true. Now that I had switched over to online classes, I'd moved closer to home and decided to take on some part-time work at the bookstore. I lived in the next town over from my parents, Mistletoe Mountain, which was, yes, the most Christmasy place in the US. But I loved it there. It was almost like having Christmas all year round.

I spent most of my time focused on classes. And when I wasn't at the bookstore, I was hanging out with my two best friends, Gretchen and Abigail. I hadn't spoken much to the few friends I'd made while I was on campus since I'd been back.

I talked with my mom a couple more minutes before I got a panicked message from Gretchen and a voice message right after that from Abigail simply stating, "Please help."

After giving my parents a quick habitual kiss on the cheek, I got in my car to leave… except the engine didn't even turn over.

My dad came out to look at the car. "I don't think it's the battery," he said as he scratched the bridge of his nose. He used to be a car guy before he got wrapped up in the bakery business with my mom, so I trusted that he knew when it wasn't an immediate fix.

I could feel the twitch of uneasiness crawl up my arms. I really, really didn't want to miss the Santa Claus Ball.

Next thing I knew, my mom was tossing a pair of keys at my head. I nearly caught the Christmas Mickey Mouse cake pop keychain right to the nose, but thankfully, I caught it.

"I'd say you can take our car, except there's no gas and it's full of supplies I need for a cake Jack promised to work on first thing."

The bakery van? I glanced outside at the red and white decaled van out front. "Guess that'll do," I said. I was quickly losing the time I'd planned to use to get ready. If I didn't leave now, I'd be late for sure.

"Thanks, Mom! I owe you! I'll work for you every day during Christmas break!" I yelled as I ran out the door.

"You better not!" my mom hollered back at me.

The twenty-minute drive went by quickly as I admired the patches of snow that had begun to collect on the sides of the road. The mix of adrenaline and long-awaited anticipation of the ball had my chest feeling tight with giddiness. I just knew it was going to be exactly as my mom described—probably minus the meeting the love of my life part.

When I pulled into the driveway of Abigail's and my little town-house, Gretchen was running out on the front porch to meet me. I couldn't tell if she was excited or panicked, but perhaps it was both.

I brushed my fingers over the silver-beaded garland we'd hung around our porch rail as I trotted up to meet her.

"Shoes! Where are your shoes?" she said, clutching my arms dramatically.

I stepped inside the door and pushed aside the extra coats and scarves hanging behind the door and pointed at the floor. Gretchen nearly fawned to the ground, thanking me with every retroactive breath she took.

Carol, my little black and gray terrier, trotted over to meet me after Gretchen ran off to situate herself. I gave Carol a little scratch on the neck, jingling the bells on her collar. She gave my hand a happy lick and retreated back to her gingerbread shaped dog house.

The rest of the time we had to get ready went smoothly, and Abigail braided my hair and helped me pull on the white wig. It probably seemed a little silly for people on the outside, but dressing up as Mrs. Claus was part of the gig, part of the tradition.

Everyone had their own take on it, and as I checked myself out in the mirror, I was satisfied with my look. I ran my hands over the flared red skirt and double-checked that the back of my diamond red earrings were on securely.

"I got the masks!" Abigail said as she clunked through the house in her white heels. "Let's get this show on the road!"

CHAPTER 2

Patrick

I couldn't be upset that Mrs. Henson had some work for me on a Saturday. She was a nice, older woman who regularly asked for my services, even the non-electric related things. But I was willing to do anything for her because not only was she a close friend of my aunt, but she had also come to feel like a grandma to me. And after her husband of fifty-five years had passed away a few months ago, I'd started to give in to even more of her requests to come out and fix whatever small problem she was having–even on a Saturday.

"I'm so sorry to have you come out again," Mrs. Henson said as she wrapped her crocheted shawl around her shoulders. "I'm afraid I just don't know how to do anything."

I noted the way she squeezed her eyebrows together with anxiety. I felt bad for her, and I didn't want her to feel guilty for depending on me. It was only natural for a partner to feel a little lost after losing the person who had been faithfully by their side for over half their life.

I gave her my best careless grin. "It's no problem at all, Beth." She'd made me start calling her by her first name within the first month.

Maybe it had something to do with the heartbreak of hearing "Mrs." and "Henson" strung together so many times.

She opened the door wide to let me in. It was chilly in this place. Yes, it was mid-November, so one might expect that, but it wasn't good for an elderly woman to be in this kind of atmosphere. She was bound to get sick.

Mrs. Henson hugged her arms tightly around herself. Under her little hand-made shawl, she was also wearing a turtle neck with a sweater over it. I glanced down at her feet, which were stuffed into a pair of fuzzy house slippers with fat, fuzzy socks puffing out the sides.

I sighed. It had been a couple of weeks since I'd seen her last, and I wondered if I didn't need to start seeing her more, even when she didn't ask.

"How's Chester doing?" I asked as she led me through her small living room into the main hallway.

"That little son of a gun is around here somewhere. You wouldn't believe what he did last night!" she said.

I grinned. Talking about her cat seemed to put her at ease. Her pinched eyebrows gave way to that classic amused and irritated expression she wore when she talked about Chester. He was an adopted orange tabby that Mrs. Henson had decided to get a couple of months after her husband's passing.

"What'd he do this time?" I asked with a smirk. "Dig up your hoya again? Scratch the curtain?"

Mrs. Henson gave a light huff. "Get this. I'm sleeping soundly–yet rather a bit coldly–in my bed. Then this little bugger comes zooming through the house and comes dashing right over me in bed!"

I set my bag down, but I had a feeling I wasn't going to need it. All she wanted me to do was adjust the thermostat. It wouldn't take me long, but I took my time as she told me stories about Chester and how John would have absolutely loved him, and all the while insisting that he hated him.

After I switched the air to heat and changed the temperature from

Celsius to Fahrenheit, I gave Beth an in-depth tutorial on how to operate her thermostat.

"I feel like a big ol' goof," she said.

I patted her on the back. "You're not a goof, Beth," I told her. "Lots of people don't know how to operate these things when they first get them. There's a learning curve no matter your age or gender or ability."

She gave me a crooked, doubting smile. "Thanks for saying that, Patrick."

I picked up my bag and started to say my goodbyes, but a bashful look came across Mrs. Henson's face and she reached out to pat my forearm.

"I'm sorry, but would you mind doing me another huge favor while you're here?" she asked, a tinge of pink coming up between the wrinkles of her cheeks. "I promise I'll pay you. I'll even pay extra since it's a Saturday and you're doing more work than you bargained for!"

I patted her cool hand. "That's not necessary," I told her, though I was beginning to wonder what time it was. I'd need to shower and get dressed before the Santa Claus Ball. I was a bit nervous to go since this was my first time going as a single man since I'd broken up with my girlfriend. This time I'd participate in the Mistletoe Mystery and potentially be matched with a date. It'd been a year since I'd dated anyone, but I thought I was ready to dip my toes back in the water. And with the Mistletoe Mystery, there was no pressure for anyone to actually date their match, so it felt like a safe enough reintroduction to the dating world.

Mrs. Henson guided me to the kitchen and pointed at the stove. She gave it a timid point. "It's not working."

I tried to switch on the stove, and she was right—no heat. I worried a bit that this one might take a bit too long to find out and fix, but I looked at the lonely, withered woman next to me and knew I couldn't leave just yet.

"How long has it been out?" I asked.

She scratched at the loose bun tied up behind her head. "Maybe about five days? I was trying to make some soup a few days ago but the stove top didn't seem to be working. I hoped that it was just the top, so I went ahead and prepared to bake some Christmas cookies for a party with your aunt, but I ended up having to take the dough to her place to bake them because the oven wasn't working either.

I nodded. "All right," I said, mentally preparing myself to get back in the work zone and push out thoughts of the Santa Claus Ball.

It took longer to work on the stove than I expected, but it turned out that since it was an older stove, we'd either have to order a part to keep it running or Mrs. Henson would have to decide if she wanted to buy a new one. But it was working for now.

"I'll have to give it some thought," she said. "The new ones are probably all fancy, and I won't know how they work either. Pretty soon I'll be living in a house that's smarter than me! I won't know how to walk through the door!"

I did my best to console Mrs. Henson and let her know that she wasn't alone, no matter how lonely she might feel. Whether she expected it or not, she pretty much had me as an adoptive son.

"Let me pay you a bit extra for your trouble," Mrs. Henson insisted. She turned around and went to grab her purse off of the kitchen table.

I gently held her hands back from her purse. "Really, Beth. Don't even think about it. It's not real work when I help you out."

She curled down the corner of her mouth, deepening her wrinkles. "Patrick…."

I chuckled. "I'm serious!"

She lightly smacked my arm. "At least let me bake you some of those Christmas cookies now that the stove is working. Let me at least use you to test it out."

"That sounds perfect," I told her.

She gave my arm a light squeeze before turning away and walking back toward the living room. I followed slowly behind her, suddenly feeling sorry that I was about to leave her alone again… except for Chester the crazy orange cat, anyway.

"Say, Beth, what are you doing tonight?" I asked her.

She slowed and twisted her neck back to face me. "Oh, I suppose I'll have some dinner with Chester and watch some more TV."

"You're not going to the Santa Claus Ball?"

She cocked her head slightly. "Is that tonight?"

I nodded.

"Well, I hadn't planned on going anyway. I don't think that's the kind of place for an old woman like me."

"Nonsense!" I said. "It's for the whole town—well, the whole county, really! And you're not that old! Going out will keep you young, I hear."

She smiled sadly. "I don't think I can handle it just yet, if I'm being honest. I wouldn't know who to talk to unless your aunt was there. And I'm not about to step on your toes and ruin your chances of meeting a younger, better-looking girl."

I gave her a stern look, but I didn't want to push her. "Well, you wouldn't be stepping on my toes unless you decided to dance with me, and in that case, it's more likely that I'd be stepping on yours. But if you're not comfortable yet, I understand."

She gave a soft, tired smile. "Thanks, hun."

I nodded and moved to step past her toward the door. Before I went out, I turned back. "Beth? Remember that there are a lot of events happening this season. I know it's hard with John gone and all, but I hope you don't keep yourself away. Please think about joining some of the festivities. And, hey, you can even be my date." I flashed a quick smile and a wink.

That got a genuine smile to come up on her face. "How could I say no to that?" she said with feigned flattery. "I'd be the most envied girl of them all."

"That's right," I told her.

Mrs. Henson glanced at the clock. "You better get out of here now," she said. "I'll get started on those cookies first thing tomorrow."

I smiled. "I'm looking forward to it."

As I made my way back home, I let my thoughts drift back to the ball. My buddy Andrew had talked me into it. He was the kind to frequent any kind of community get-together so he could meet ladies.

He was the suave type, a borderline playboy. But he at least had more respect for them than some other guys. I suspected this was because of his close relationship with his mom.

Regardless of Andrew's convincing, I was starting to look forward to this party. Of course, I was hesitant to get back into the dating scene, but he kept reminding me that tonight didn't have to be the start of anything other than me going back out into society.

It was ironic that going out into that society, at least in this case, required hiding behind a mask. It was only temporary, the mask thing, but I thought it was amusing.

After I finally returned to my end of town and cleaned up in the shower, I did my best to shape up my stubble and trim the bits of hair that tickled the tops of my ears. I slipped on the velvety red suit that Andrew had helped me pick out. It felt strange wearing a suit, and a bright-colored flashy one at that. But I had to admit that Andrew had impeccable taste and that I looked good.

On the other hand, I wasn't confident I could pull off the white beard and tiny rounded glasses. So I tugged on the beard and fixed the Santa hat securely to my head. I decided to save the glasses for once I arrived because seeing out of them was surprisingly tricky, and they'd be above my mask anyway.

Before stepping out of the house and pretty much jogging to my truck, I shot Andrew a message that I'd meet him in the library parking lot next to the auditorium. With the low rumble of my truck's engine coming to life, my nerves spiked. I was really doing this. I felt a little ridiculous and a little thrilled, a little anxious, and a little full of myself. It was hard telling how this night was going to go.

CHAPTER 3

Holly

"I CAN'T BELIEVE we showed up to this thing in a cookie on wheels," Gretchen said. She wasn't all for riding to her potential engagement in my parent's bakery van. It wasn't the most romantic car in the world, but it was the only option that would fit the three of us since mine was temporarily out of commission, Abigail drove a little 2013 Mazda Miata with only two seats, and Gretchen didn't want to take her car since she planned to leave with Joey for a midnight showing of A Christmas Story.

"Get over it, girl," Abigail told her with a tough love tone. "If you really love him, you won't care what kind of car you arrive at your engagement in."

Gretchen frowned with a little sad sigh. "Yeah, yeah. You might have a point."

We all stepped out of the car, helping each other fix our hair and masks.

I wrapped my arm around Gretchen's shoulders and gave her a light squeeze. "G, to be honest, you gotta let go. You've been so caught up in wondering if he's going to propose or not that you're not focusing on the moment. Your fixation is going to take away from simply having a good time."

Gretchen was silent for a moment, staring down at her shoes—well, my shoes.

Abigail came up to Gretchen's other side and hooked her finger under her chin. "Look up, G. You're already missing the party!"

Gretchen finally lifted her face to the auditorium where her eyes slowly drank in the wonder. I took the moment to study the decorations and the lights, too, as a feeling of awe from the magical scene filled my chest.

Along the way to the auditorium we'd seen everyone's regular home decorations and the lights strung across the storefronts, and that was all beautiful and wonderful, but the Santa Claus Ball was different. Though I'd seen this place decorated every year of my life I could remember– except last year– this year felt especially magical.

Over the man-made tunnel leading into the auditorium, beams of light flashed into the sky as if to say, "This is the epicenter of Christmas!" Out front, literal candy cane lanes guided people past decorations on the lawn. There was Santa's sleigh–a real, antique sleigh–painted a pristine crimson and trimmed with gold. The intricate swirl designs on the hood were stunning. In a small fenced-in field were nine real reindeer, each with beautiful Nordic harnesses. Each of the reindeer's harnesses depicted their names–Dasher, Dancer, Prancer, Vixen, Comet, Cupid, Donner, Blitzen, and, of course, Rudolph. When I was a kid, I'd make my mom let me feed each one of them a little carrot or an apple slice out of my hand. The feeling of their slobbering, wet tongues were still fresh in my mind.

The freshly fallen snow was truly helping to set the mood, the lights hitting it casting a beautiful, clean glow. And even as we stepped inside the entryway, a slew of fake snow blanketed the sides of the walkway, and crystal snowflakes hung from the ceiling. The auditorium's stage was set up beautifully as a scene from A Christmas Carol, set with the enchanting warm glow of a hundred lightbulbs seemingly floating in the air, with a quartet of strings and an accordion playing music right in the middle of it. I'd always loved the book, and I was excited to see parts of it living right in front of me. The auditorium was beautiful, but that wasn't where the Santa Claus Ball shined. That happened right around the corner behind the stage in the ballroom.

Several other "Mr. and Mrs. Clauses" filed in or mingled by the entryway, talking about the lights or the music. I spotted one tall Santa Claus and wondered if he could be my match later tonight. It was getting more thrilling to think about as we neared the ballroom.

I squeezed my friends' hands as we stepped into the magical world that was Santa Claus' Ball. From the tall ceilings hung several golden chandeliers, and again the ceiling was adorned with the warm glow of lights. A magnificently tall Christmas tree stole my attention from the corner of the room. It was decorated with giant intricate Christmas balls, silver tinsel, and beautiful vintage ornaments. Red bows were tied here and there, and a giant crystal star shone at the top of the tree. There was a smattering of wrapped-up presents under the tree, prizes for drawings and games. Each window around the room was affixed with garland and little pinecones and ribbons. The tables surrounding the dance floor glowed with charming golden candelabras and classic Nordic tableware.

And in the middle of the space, where people would waltz the night away, was the dance floor. It was trimmed with a circle of freshly fallen fake snow, and hundreds of mistletoe branches hung from sparkling golden strings.

This was it. This was the year I'd step onto the dance floor and find a match. I'd dance and chat with the men in the dance circle for approximately thirty minutes before having to make a final decision. If my choice also chose me, we'd share a kiss at midnight under that mistletoe and remove our masks.

That was the tradition in Mistletoe Mountain. I thought it just came from the town founders' strong idealism that nobody should be alone on Christmas and Christmas was a time to find and share love, to kindle relationships, and to let magic happen. But I wasn't sure that was really the case, but it made sense to me. So, every Saturday after

Thanksgiving for the last two hundred-odd years, we kicked off Christmas with the Santa Claus Ball, complete with games, dancing, plays, carriage rides, and the Mistletoe Mystery.

One beauty of this match-making phenomenon was that as part of the tradition, every person who attended the ball had to dress as Santa or Mrs. Claus, and possibly since this event started, people also had to wear masks–until midnight, that was. So as it was, we were all free to roam about and chat, but unless we recognized someone by their voice, we probably wouldn't know who we were talking to. This thought used to make me nervous, but now I thought it was a sweet sentiment–getting to know people, especially a potential love match, by conversation and chemistry alone.

As I thought about it, my tummy somersaulted with excitement.

When I was a young girl, I garnered an innocent admiration for this event called the Mistletoe Mystery. My mother had spoken of it so fondly and painted the beauty of it so vividly because of her experience with my father.

But that innocence waned for a while as I reached my teenage years. I thought it was weird that everyone was cool with kissing strangers. But then, this year, that original child-like awe crept back into my heart. Perhaps I truly had taken up my mother's hopeless romanticism.

"Wait!" Abigail shouted suddenly, stopping us all near an ice sculpture of a vintage Santa.

I flinched at the unexpected sound.

"Jeez, what was that for?" Gretchen whined. "You scared the gumdrops out of me!"

I smirked. When Gretchen wasn't being anxious or obsessive, she could be a little funny.

Abigail took a moment to shove her hand down into her purse, elbow deep, and dig around. I watched with curiosity while Gretchen looked on with vexation until Abigail finally revealed the treasure from the bottom of her purse.

She held out her hand, showing three vintage brooches. "I know we know who we are right now, but maybe this'll make it a bit easier to spot each other if and when we get separated."

Gretchen chose the white diamond broach, while I was more attracted to the emerald. It was set in a golden swirling diamond shape. That left Abigail with the red one.

"That's the one I wanted anyway," she said with a smug smile.

Shortly after our arrival, around eight o'clock, the party was already in full swing. Gretchen managed to find Joey in the chaos of Clauses, and we didn't see much of them. Abigail and I stuck together most of the time, visiting with small groups of men who approached us. Some tried to guess who we were, but we opted to play by the rules and not give in to their questioning.

It was a nice evening. The music swelled around us, the aroma of cinnamon and apples and popcorn filled our noses. I remained mesmerized by the lights, some of which were programmed to change and flash with the music.

I was tuning out a conversation between Abigail and a Santa when someone announced that those wanting to participate in the Mistletoe Mystery were to make their way to the dance floor, men on the north side and women on the south side. They reminded us we'd have thirty minutes of continuous dancing, switching every two minutes for the first twenty minutes, and then ten minutes at the end to find our chosen match before the kiss.

My stomach was fluttering wildly. I'd have my first kiss in years in only thirty minutes–if everything went as planned. But, what exactly was the plan? What if I really did meet someone great?

I didn't have time to think about it as I made my way to the dance floor with at least fifty other people. It was a bit overwhelming, but I was in it. I was–mostly–ready.

I tried to scan the crowd of Santa Clauses, and something in my mind made me let out a giggle. This was hilarious, going on speed dates with a bunch of people dressed as the same magical old dude.

My gaze was suddenly trapped by the observant watch of a slender, tall statured man in a velvety red suit. I thought I saw his fake white beard twitch. Was that a smile? My heart flitted in my chest. *He was looking at me, right?* Suddenly, I was overcome with nerves.

But I didn't have time to react because the DJ tapped on the microphone and began counting down from three. At the sharp ding of the bell, the dance floor was filled with urgency. The hurried clack of heels passed me as men and women sought out their first match straight across from them.

My first match met me and bowed slightly. "Good night," he said formally. "Or, ah, how is your night going?" he asked.

I looked him over. He wasn't the man who'd caught my attention before the bell rang. He was tall but skinnier. His fake beard was longer and his mask was matte satin.

"It's such a beautiful night," I said, returning his bow with a small nod.

He gestured at my hands and I lifted them up to meet him.

"I guess this is the part where we start dancing," I said awkwardly.

The man's hands were clammy and warm. I supposed I couldn't blame him. Mine probably were, too.

I tried to think of something to say, but my first match ended up being totally silent. After that, I didn't have much luck for the first few matches. The conversation was awkward or forced or nonexistent, and with one guy, I didn't have the chance to speak at all.

I was about to give up and accept that I wouldn't have the same luck as my mother when the bell dinged and everyone switched partners again. I felt the velvety finish of the suit in my hands first after automatically opening my arms to receive my next dance partner. I looked up to see the same creamy white mask embroidered with holly branches and golden swirls that I had been attracted to earlier. I let my hands settle on his sturdy arm while he clasped the other confidently.

"Ah," he said. "It's you."

He spoke with a relaxed, soothing baritone voice. I was a bit dazed by it, even though it barely cut through the chatter around us. Apparently, a lot of these people were better at having conversations than I was.

It must have been because my answer was too slow, but the velvet-suited man felt the need to clarify.

"I saw you earlier, laughing. I was just curious what it was about," he said.

I let him lead me in the dance and let myself focus on my response instead. I tried to relax under his watchful gaze.

"I was just wondering if anyone else thought it was a little silly that we're all dressed up like old people trying to get dates," I said.

The white mustache twitched again. Another smile? I wondered what it looked like… did he have dimples? Was it a toothy smile or closed-lipped?

"You're not into older men?" the velvet-suited man asked.

I had to smirk. "I'm into magical men."

The man snorted and tightened his grip on my hand. "That's a high bar, but I respect it."

I smiled again, and he studied my mouth, once again making me a bit self-conscious. I knew he wouldn't be able to see my whole face, as half of it was obstructed by my mask. I hid my face on his shoulder.

"You don't need to hide from me," he said. I could feel his hand move up slightly on my back.

"Don't you think that's a bit ironic?" I said. "We're all hiding."

"But not forever," he said. This man had a confident air about him that I really appreciated. "Just until midnight." I could hear a teasing lilt in his voice that made me want to smile again.

I decided to look up at him one more time.

"I hope I get to see you," he said.

My heart faltered. *Did that mean…?*

But before I let myself question it, the words were out. "I want to see you, too."

And before he could respond, the bell dinged, signaling our time to switch partners.

"Let's meet again," he said before letting go of me.

Before I knew it, I'd been swept up by another mystery man. I wondered how much longer we had. How would I find him again in this crowd of people?

Fortunately, we were notified of our last dance after one more switch. I tried not to be disrespectful of the man I was dancing with, but he caught me glancing around, and I wasn't very responsive to his attempts at starting a conversation.

"Did you already find the one?" he asked. He wasn't mad or sad. It was more of a simple statement.

I hesitated before realizing that I was being a little rude. "Sorry," I apologized automatically.

The guy shrugged. "I get it. I think I'm already in love with the girl I first danced with."

I smiled at this lighthearted honesty. "Really? Your connection was that strong?"

I could feel him radiating a grin in front of me. "Maybe so."

"I hope it works out for you," I told him sincerely.

The guy nodded his head in another direction and leaned in to whisper in my ear. "And for you, too. Seems like someone can't take their eyes off of you."

I glanced over my shoulder, but I couldn't get a good look over the people between us. I was about to make another comment when the bell made its final ding. My current dance partner said, "Good luck," and slid off across the floor.

The circle of the dance floor was filled with urgency as people shouted nicknames or codewords or as they held up symbols with their hands so their other half could find them easily. I kicked myself for not having thought of something like that. I also kicked myself for not wearing my taller heels.

I wasn't sure how much time passed as people tried to find their chosen matches, but I was beginning to worry I wouldn't find the velvet-suited man in time, or worse yet, he could have chosen someone else....

Just then, a strong hand caught hold of my arm and gently turned me around. "There you are," he said.

CHAPTER 4

Patrick

My heart raced as I placed my hand on her shoulder. I'd been trying
to keep my eye on her so I wouldn't lose her in the crowd of dancing
Clauses and Mrs. Clauses. Every time I lost her, I'd find that shining
emerald brooch on her dress. It hadn't let me down yet.

She relaxed. I breathed a sigh of relief. "I thought maybe you had
found someone else," she said timidly. I barely heard her over the
muttering of the other people on the dance floor.

I trailed my hand down her arm to take hold of her hand.

"Two minutes!" the DJ called out.

Just in time, I thought.

Two minutes until the kiss…. I was still nervous, but growing
more excited.

"There's something about you," I told her.

The DJ piped up on the mic again. "Just a reminder, if you found
the match you want to kiss, you'd better give them a squeeze so
nobody takes them away!"

"Well, we'd hate that now, wouldn't we?" I said, wrapping my arms around her back and hoping that I wasn't going to make her uncomfortable. But she linked her arms through mine loosely. I was happy to know that she was feeling the same way as me about this surprising encounter. It felt so intimate and secure at the same time.

"This is so weird," she said with a laugh. She glanced around at some of the other couples around us. Some looked excited while others looked somewhere closer to anxious. I was bordering on the precipice of both.

"We don't have to really kiss if you're not comfortable with it," I whispered near her ear.

She could probably barely hear me because of the noise from everyone else around us. And every second of she stood in silence, the sound of my heart pounding in my ears grew louder and louder. She glanced up at the hundreds of mistletoe hanging above us. I looked too.

"Well, you know what the tradition says," she said quietly, though I wasn't sure I had heard her properly.

The DJ piped up one final time to give us a countdown. The kissing would commence in four, three....

"Really, I don't want you to feel pressured," I said again, looking down at her.

She glanced up at me, and I couldn't help but admire at her bright red lips.

Two, one....

The bell rang, and she rose up on the very tips of her toes and pressed her lips to mine. She caught me by surprise, causing me let out a little gasp before I got it in my mind to kiss her back. I went time-blind as she relaxed into our kiss and tightened her arm around my back.

The bell dinged again, causing us to break away.

"Wow! Can you feel the magic in the air, everyone?" the DJ said over the mic.

We broke away, and embarrassment flooded through me. I was almost glad when she hid her face in my shoulder once again. It was cute that she did that, though I worried she could hear my heart thumping fast. Absentmindedly, I let out two short chuckles. She was right. This was strange, but I liked it.

"It's time, everyone!" the DJ prompted. "Time for the reveal. On zero, you can take off your masks."

Suddenly, I was becoming nervous again. What would we do after this, after sharing a beautiful kiss with a stranger? I didn't know what she looked like. I didn't know what she'd think of me when I removed my mask and this dreaded scratchy beard. At least I'd had enough sense to pick one of the short ones that didn't get in the way when I was eating, or when I was kissing....

"Are you ready?" I asked her.

Even though I didn't expect this and I didn't know what was supposed to come after it, I had a strange, magical sense that I was indeed ready to see her.

She nodded, and I hoped she was telling the truth. Suddenly, she wasn't looking up at me anymore.

"Let's count together, everyone!" the DJ called out.

The rest of the crowd began from ten and started counting down slowly.

I knew it might be pushing it, but I hooked my finger gently under her chin and urged her to look up. She pressed her lips together. I hoped she wasn't already regretting this whole thing.

Five, four....

I lifted my hands to my mask and she did the same.

Three, two....

The fire alarm rang through the ballroom, echoing off of the walls and drowning out the music and the chatter. And in a matter of seconds, the room was fueled with panic and chaos.

"Hold on," I told her, taking her hand in mine.

She took it without hesitation. "My friend..." she said, her voice barely audible.

Some people were shouting and calling out for their friends and family. The staff of the party were trying to control the crowd and get everyone to move toward the doors. But people were surprised and in a panic. They pushed their way through, desperate to get out.

I scanned the room to see if there were any signs of fire, but I didn't see anything yet. Still, it was safer to get out now.

Suddenly, someone slammed into me, nearly knocking me off my feet. I stumbled back and lost my grip on my match's hand. I swiveled around to see where she had gone, but everybody looked the same in those dang costumes.

I walked briskly along with the other party guests heading toward the exit, but I couldn't find her. I looked for the green pin on the white collar of her dress again, but I could only see most people's backs. As I scanned the crowd, I saw an older lady get knocked down. She fell into one of the tables, nearly tipping the candle over. I caught the candle and blew it out and reached out for the lady.

"Come with me," I told her.

She nodded and grabbed onto my arm. I did my best to brace her as we slowly made it outside. Some people were beginning to abandon their masks, and I wondered if I'd already scanned her face without even knowing.

"I saw someone pull the fire alarm!" I heard some explain as I passed by them. "Then they just ran away! They didn't even give us a warning!"

"Will you be okay?" I asked the older lady. She nodded and thanked me.

I searched feverishly for my match. I hoped she was okay. I even considered going back inside to look for her, but my mind reasoned with my heart and I settled on looking for her outside instead. I wasn't sure how long I searched for her, but it was long enough that the fire department came and told us that it was a false alarm. There was no fire.

I was about to see her face, but we'd gotten separated for nothing. I pressed my lips together with frustration. And now I couldn't even find—

A glimmer of light caught my attention.

It was her….

"Bless that brooch!" I muttered aloud as I took off in her direction.

She was still wearing her mask, but it was definitely her–the mid-thigh length red dress with the faux fur trimming the bottom and the collar, the long red sleeves that split at the ends to reveal the slenderness of her wrists, that red bottom lip... and the emerald diamond-shaped pin.

I opened my mouth to call out to her, but my voice halted in my throat. I didn't know her name. I should have thought of some clever nickname like some of the other couples on the dance floor had done, but the idea never crossed my mind. Our time together was too short, and oh, so unexpected.

Some other woman dressed as Mrs. Claus came up to her. They spoke for a moment and then the woman grabbed her hand and led her away, into the parking lot. My match looked over her shoulder.

Was she looking for me?

I felt hope spring up in my chest, but it crashed when she turned around and hurried away with her friend. I continued to try to get to her, but swimming through the crowd proved to be very difficult. I barely caught sight of her getting into the driver's side of a large red and green van before she disappeared.

The van backed up and began to drive away. I made sure to take note of the image on the side, a giant gingerbread cookie on a Christmas plate. The name... the name... something about Kringle? I didn't quite catch it before it drove out of sight.

Things slowly began to calm down, so I got ahold of my buddy Andrew to make sure he was okay. He'd already been outside when the fire alarm went off, so he wasn't really in danger in the first place. When I learned that everything was clear and there was nothing I could do to help, I went back to my little pickup and pulled up a search engine on my phone. I typed in all sorts of variations of "bakery" and "Kringle" until I was certain I found the one–Kris Kringle's Cookies. It was in the next town over, Noel. I'd been there once or twice, but it was too far for this time of night considering nobody would be there at... nearly two AM.

I pinned the location on my maps feature and drove home.

As I laid in bed, tossing and turning, I couldn't stop thinking about what my match looked like, about how her hand felt in mine, the quiet shyness in her voice amid all the other couples. I wanted to hear her voice again, without all the extra sound. I wanted to hear the giggle that matched the magical way she shined when she laughed. Something about her drew me in.

And just when I thought I was reading into the electricity buzzing between us, she so confidently stood on her toes to kiss me....

I gulped. Never in my life had I literally had my breath taken away like that before.

I knew I needed to find her again.

I WAS SURPRISED any bakery would be open on a Sunday, but Kris Kringle's Cookies certainly was, and it was packed. Cars lined up outside and people were heading toward their vehicles with arm loads of cookies and desserts.

I looked around for evidence of the van that I had seen the night before, but I didn't see anything. So, I gathered up a bit of courage and strode inside.

The door dinged when I entered and a man probably ten years older than me greeted me as he pressed a box of what I assumed was cookies toward his customer. The sound of old-timey Christmas songs played over the speakers in the background. It was a cute little bakery, and it did smell delicious.

"How can I help you?" the man asked.

I placed my hand on the counter, wishing I had given my speech a little more planning. "I'm sorry to ask such a random question, but I'm looking for someone."

The man's smile began to sag a little. He looked at me with uncertainty.

"Sorry," I said again. "It's a young woman. I, uh, met her at the Santa Claus Ball last night. I didn't catch her name because the fire alarm went off and I lost sight of her, but I saw her drive off in a bakery van that I thought belonged to this place...."

The man's smile had lit back up. In fact, he might have been laughing on the inside. "I have to say I've never heard a story quite like that before," he said. "It's straight out of Cinderella's world."

I could feel the embarrassment creeping in and my neck began to feel hot. I rubbed the back of my neck. "It doesn't seem real to me either."

"I wish I could help you," the guy said. "But I don't think it was our van. We only drive it for deliveries. And we don't have any young women who work for us. It's just me and the older couple that runs this place."

My heart sank a little. "Man, I was sure it belonged to this place," I said.

"Well, there are a couple of other bakeries with similar vans to ours in the area. We've all got them decorated to advertise for a Christmas fundraiser for the elderly in nursing homes and those who don't have anyone to spend the holidays with," he explained.

That was nice, I thought as I remembered Mrs. Henson. "Well, then," I said. I glanced over into the glass that was filled with cookies and cakes. "I'll take a few of your best cookies to support your cause."

The man smiled and gathered a few, explaining that the short-bread and gingerbread were particularly popular this time of year. "And I'll toss in a free classic Kris Kringle sugar cookie just for you."

I paid and thanked him for the trouble. As I turned to leave, I spotted an older couple coming out from the back room. I nodded to them and said thank you and Merry Christmas. They smiled and waved as I turned to leave.

I got into my truck and just thought for a moment. Even if she hadn't gotten into this particular van, it sounded like every other bakery in town might have had a similar design for the season, so I knew I might just have to go to every single one of them to find her. I was sure she was somewhere in this town, and I was going to figure out a way to find her.

CHAPTER 5

Holly

IT WAS ALL I could do not to think about him all weekend. Actually, I was sure I'd failed at it because every time I saw a man on the street or in a restaurant or sitting in the car next to me at the stoplights, I wondered if it was him. I found myself on two occasions wearing the same shoes I'd worn that night so I could compare my height to the men I walked by. I started to feel pretty pathetic about it, actually.

It was just one kiss, after all. I was sure there were a lot of other people at the party who were in the same boat as me. The fire alarm was unexpected, to say the least, but being pulled away from him like that—it was like someone was trying to snuff out a Christmas miracle.

I was angry at the person who'd pulled the fire alarm, for whatever reason they had. Since there was no reason, I assumed it was mischief, probably some high school kids thinking they were being funny. But because of them or whoever it was, I didn't know his face. I couldn't trust anything I remembered about the color of his eyes with the impediment of the mask and the shining lights all around us. Even the sound of his voice was foggy. All I remembered was that it was soothing.

"Are you going to mope around the house today or get yourself together?" Abigail asked.

She was always the tough-love type, the straight shooter.

I glared at her. "I have *not* been moping," I said firmly.

Abigail switched off the TV. "You never turn on the TV at–" She glanced at her watch. "Eight-twelve?" She stared at me in disbelief. "Besides, how many times have you watched *White Christmas* now?"

She had a point. I had already played it through three times. This was the start of my fourth.

"I'm not moping," I insisted. "I just don't have any plans today."

Abigail rolled her eyes. "You are not the kind of person that doesn't have plans at any point during the Christmas season. Let me see your book."

On the end table next to me was my little daily planner. Yearly, I filled it with stickers and drawings and filled up my days in fifteen minute time slots. She snatched the book off the table before I could protest. She stabbed a pointed finger into one of the pages and then showed it to me.

"See?" she said. "According to this, you should be reading to kids at the bookstore in an hour!"

Honestly, I had forgotten I had planned to go in early before work for that. I stood from the couch and grabbed my journal out of her hand. "Yes, I know. I've been out every day. So, like I said, I'm not moping. I'm still doing most of the things."

She narrowed her eyes at me in disbelief. "But if you don't do every single thing on that list, that leads me to believe it's half-hearted. That's moping by my standards."

"Fine!" I said. I was less annoyed that she was getting onto me than I was that she was right. It was silly to let some velvet-dressed mystery man ruin my Christmas plans just because every time I went out I was less sure I'd ever find him again.

Abigail came over to me and hooked her arm over my shoulders. This was her version of a hug. "Girl, let's go out. Let's meet up with G and do all these things on your list! Christmas is your favorite time of year. Don't let this little blip in time keep you from enjoying the season."

It was sweet that she was trying to get me back in the right head-space. I'd kind of forgotten that I could count on her for things like this. I swiveled around and surprised her with a hug. "You're right, Abby. Let's get out of here and have some fun."

Abigail gently pushed me away–she wasn't much of a hugger. But she smiled at me with a mischievous grin. "Besides," she said, "have you even bothered to look outside this morning?"

She nodded to the window and I ran over to it.

"It snowed!" I yelled. "Like a lot!"

The night of the Santa Claus Ball had brought a few inches of snow, but as usual, all Mistletoe Mountain needed to do was hit the first of December before she pulled out the big guns. There had to be at least two feet of snow on the ground, and it was still falling, albeit slowly.

"I knew that'd get you going," Abigail said. "And I already called G. She'll be here at three o'clock sharp this afternoon, or maybe ten after on account of the weather. So you better get in the shower. And... do something with your hair."

Her look was borderline judgy, but I probably deserved it. But not anymore. I was going to get my act together today. It was December first, it was snowing, and I had plans.

But first, I had to go to work. No, first, I had to take a shower.

I KEPT STARING out the window at the snow falling, and the nearer it got to three o'clock, the more excited I felt to get off work and get back into the swing of things. I was grateful Abigail had lovingly dragged me out of the house that morning and barely got me to the bookstore on time. Once I arrived and got into the second Christmas book reading with the kids, I was starting to feel that warm and tingly feeling that Christmas always gave me.

I had even taken the time to reschedule some of the activities I had skipped over the last couple of days. The next thing on the list for the day was to start decorating the park.

Despite the town's name and love for Christmas, Mistletoe Mountain didn't jump over all the other holidays and whip out the Christmas stuff in September like a lot of the commercial stores. Heading up to Thanksgiving, you would see evidence here and there of winter themes, but aside from the Santa Claus Ball and a few overzealous town members digging out their own decorations, December first was *the* day to deck the halls, or rather, the street, with Christmas.

Every year, a couple groups of volunteers would tackle the three parks around town and start hanging up Christmas ornaments and lights. Sometimes I wondered if I didn't actually enjoy this more than the Santa Claus Ball because after that day, everywhere you turned in town was Christmas.

When three o'clock hit, I was out the door and headed to the park where Abigail and Gretchen would meet me, along with a handful of other volunteers to get started on Yule Park.

There were already at least three people there when I arrived–a couple of men and one woman–pulling decorations out of one of the city vans. Seeing all the colorful ornaments made me even more excited to get started decorating. I didn't even wait for Gretchen and Abigail before I stepped in to help.

We started by putting boxes of ornaments near the evergreens that were littered through the park, leaving them there until whoever was bringing the lights showed up so we could string those on first. Next, we worked on sorting out the parts for the animated Santa's sleigh and reindeer decoration, which was more complicated than it seemed. By the time we got everything sorted, Abigail and Gretchen arrived.

"I tried to get her here sooner," Abigail told me. "You know how she gets when her hat doesn't match her boots."

I rolled my eyes and gave Gretchen a sympathetic pat on the back. She wasn't the laborer type, but for the last couple of years, Abigail and I had dragged her along to help set up the decorations in whatever park we were assigned to.

One of the volunteers named Andrew had been cracking jokes the whole time. He was a suave and charismatic guy who led me to believe he was a bit of a ladies' man. When he caught sight of Abigail, he fell silent and more serious, but he kept glancing over at her.

"Where's Pat at?" he asked one of the other volunteers. "I thought he would be here thirty minutes ago. We need help getting this sleigh together."

Abigail frowned. "Sorry, but my friends and I have been putting these decorations together for three years now. Last year we even did it by ourselves. So don't assume that just because we're a couple of good-looking women we can't lift heavy things and attach a few nuts and bolts."

Andrew blinked at her, but it was hard to tell exactly what he was thinking. "I wasn't trying to assume…."

Gretchen raised her hand. "You assumed correctly about me at least," she said. "I'm just here for the easy stuff."

I started to laugh, but another man came up to the group. "Andi, are you upsetting one of these ladies already?" he said, playfully smacking his friend on the back.

He was tall and lean but sturdy-looking. The way his thighs fit his jeans could only mean he was packing some muscles under that sheep-skin lined jacket. He had light, sandy brown hair that was long enough to curl up slightly on the ends. And his eyes were that shining royal shade of blue that you could find hidden deep in a fresh drift of snow.

Andrew ignored the comment and instead turned the focus to his friend. "Dude, you were supposed to be here thirty minutes ago."

"Mrs. Henson called again."

Andrew didn't say anything else after that.

"Well, sorry I'm a little late, everyone," the man said to the group. "My name's Patrick. I'm excited to work with all of you, and you'll be happy to know I brought the most important addition to the decorations—the lights!"

Patrick....

Well, he seemed like a nice guy. He was friendly and had a winning smile. Abigail caught me staring as he turned around to grab the big bundle of lights from the back of his truck. She elbowed me in the side. "Don't just stare. Go help him out!" I didn't miss the wink she threw my way.

I cleared my throat. *What was she winking about?* I straightened up my coat and pulled my gloves on a bit tighter as I neared him.

"Need a hand?" I asked.

He seemed surprised that someone had offered help. But he just smiled and nodded. "That'd be great. Thanks."

I hefted a big looped bundle of lights while Patrick easily grabbed all the rest, his arms looping through the centers of them.

"What's your name?" he asked.

Even though I'd just cleared my throat on the way, my name had come out a little squeaky. "Holly."

"Holly?"

I nodded.

He smiled again and my heart thumped once. He was going to have to stop doing that. "I like that," he said. "Very Christmassy."

I laughed because he didn't know half of it. "Actually, my last name is Garland, so...."

He puffed out a short chuckle. "Well, that's even better then!"

I gave a lopsided, half-hearted smile. "Tell that to all of the high schoolers who always told me my parents were trying too hard."

Patrick just shrugged. "Ah, high schoolers are just rude like that. They've got the whole hormonal thing on top of the peer pressure to look cool thing. I wouldn't get hung up on that."

"At the time, I'd wished my name to be Jane Doe instead, but I'm over it now," I told him. I didn't want him to think I cared that much. I liked my name now.

I set down my string of lights on a little tarp near the base of the first tree. "Jane Doe?"

"Yeah, yeah," I said. "I was a moody high schooler too. What? You were a perfect, straight-A, All-State athlete who always donated the most to the canned food drive?"

Patrick let out a genuine laugh. The sound was deep and hearty, and it made me lose my train of thought. "Would you be upset if I told you you were right?"

I narrowed my eyes at him.

"Only eighty percent right," he said. "Timothy Jenkins always beat me at the canned food drive. People praised him for winning our class a pizza party. But I could never win against him." He stared off longingly.

I chuckled and whacked him on the arm before I remembered I'd just met this man moments ago. "Sorry," I said, tucking my hands in my pockets.

"Don't be," he said with a slightly crooked smile. "I deserved it. Maybe now's the time to tell you I wasn't any good at drama."

"Had me fooled," I muttered, turning around to return to the group. By now, we'd dropped off the last string at the farthest tree.

He chuckled again, softly this time. "You know what," he said, quickly catching up to me and walking by my side. "Usually Andrew helps me with the lights, but… I think you'd make better company."

I tried not to let my heart lift too much. After all, I was still on the lookout for my magical mystery man from the dance. But I liked Patrick. He was lighthearted and kind. He was clever and patient. We didn't get to talk as much because he had to help with the sleigh assembly first. He and two other men pieced it together while the rest of the volunteers strung out the electrical cords and got the animation working.

Toward the end of the day, Patrick and I found ourselves working side-by-side stringing the lights on some of the trees, just as he'd promised. We noted Abigail and Andrew's interaction and laughed with each other.

Patrick was good company. I found myself feeling a little sad that he wasn't the guy I was looking for. But I let myself have fun with him and with everyone else.

Everyone agreed that Gretchen should get to flip the switch to turn all the lights on, so she did. The park looked beautiful. The whole volunteer group found ourselves standing around chatting until Andrew said something catty and one of the other guys threw a clump of snow at him. It didn't take long for it to erupt into a snowball fight.

We went at it for several minutes, and by the end, we were all laughing and breathless, and Patrick declared he and I and Abigail as champions. As we cleaned up and things started to die down, I saw a woman approach Patrick. She was tall and thin with long wavy black hair. She was beautiful.

And she was smiling at him, touching his arm and acting bashful.

Of course he wasn't single. He was charming and handsome. *It was too bad,* I thought. *I might have asked him out.*

Well, at least I still had my mystery man to find.

CHAPTER 6

Patrick

EMILY'S WAS the last face I wanted to see. I'd been having such a good time with the other volunteers and the intriguing woman.

I honestly hadn't thought about Emily since before the Santa Claus Ball. I'd been too focused on trying to find my mistletoe match. I'd checked all three bakeries in the next town over to no avail. Of course, it didn't help that I didn't have a description of the woman I was looking for. All I knew was she was about five-foot-nine in heels and she was between twenty-one and twenty-five per the Santa Claus Ball's rules for the first round of the Mistletoe Mystery.

I should have known that Emily was going to pop back into my life again after I decided to get back in the dating world. She and I had been broken up for a year now, but she still weaseled her way back to me at least once a month. She'd probably heard from one of my friend's friends that I attended the Santa Claus Ball and wanted to make sure that I hadn't met anyone else.

"What do you want?" I asked her, all the joy that had been built up in me melting at the sight of her smug little smile.

I used to think it was cute when she clung to me or when she acted innocent and frail. But it didn't take long to realize it was just an act. And I wasn't falling for it anymore.

"Why do you say that every time you see me?" she asked, touching my arm.

My initial reaction was to turn and walk away, but I looked over my shoulder to see a couple of the other volunteers still hanging around. I didn't want to cause a scene in the middle of the parking lot, but I couldn't help but flinch away from her touch. I couldn't trust her anymore. I had no desire to be in her presence or to hear the gaslighting and the fishing for compliments that always came from being around Emily.

"I thought you might like that I wore my hair like this," she said, pulling her hand through it and tossing it behind her shoulder. "You couldn't keep your eyes off of me when I wore it down and kept it long like this."

I crossed my arms and stared over her head at the muddy bumper of the cars in the background.

"Well, no matter," she said. Even though I wasn't looking at her, I could feel the effort she was putting into her smile to try to appear charming. "It's been a while since I saw you and I was around, so I thought I'd surprise you with a visit."

I sighed and closed my eyes. I truly didn't understand why she thought this tactic would work on me anymore.

"What?" she asked with feigned innocence. "I'm not allowed to want to see you?"

I crossed my arms even tighter across my chest. "How did you find out I was here anyway?" I asked.

The corner of her mouth twitched wickedly. She really had no shame. "You know I have connections," she said offhandedly. Like that was supposed to impress me.

"Just tell me why you're here."

Emily's smile collapsed a bit. "I already told you. I wanted to see you."

I shook my head. I needed to really start putting my foot down if I was ever going to get rid of her. "It's been a year, Emily. You have to start leaving me alone."

She scoffed. "The biggest mistake I ever made was letting you walk away from me," she said, rubbing my bicep and sliding her hand over my shoulder.

I stepped away again. "That was my decision," I said firmly. "You didn't *let me* do anything. I chose to walk away from you because of the liar you are."

She pressed her lined lips in a straight line and stared at me fiercely. It seemed like she wasn't going to make this easy.

"Just go home," I told her before she could say anything else.

"I want to talk," she said quickly with that whine that I used to find adorable.

"There's nothing left to talk about. Let me move on." I stared straight at her. "You need to move on."

Emily crossed her arms. "With who?"

"With anyone else!" I said, accidentally raising my voice a little.

She huffed. "Not me. You. Who is it that you want to 'move on' with?" she asked with finger quotes.

The first woman that crossed my mind was my mystery mistletoe match. I'd been trying so hard the last few days to find her. And now there was this funny, intriguing volunteer. There were good women out there, right? Surely they weren't all like Emily. I wasn't sure how I had gotten trapped with Emily for so long, but I wanted to be rid of her. As far as I was concerned, she was fossilized into the previous year.

"Just go home," I repeated, choosing not to engage. If I had mentioned anyone, she would have probably taken that opportunity to find a new target or a new digging point.

She curled up her nose. "You loved me once," she said. "You'll love me again."

Apparently she didn't know that I was a different man then. Now I was stronger. I had more self-respect. I wasn't naive anymore.

After staring me down for a solid silent minute, she swiveled on her heel and left. I waited until I saw her get in her car and drive away before I went back to see if any of the volunteer group was still there.

One guy, Jason, was loading the extra stuff into one of the city vehicles. "Is anyone else left?" I asked.

He shook his head. "I think they all took off about five minutes ago."

Another woman to an interruption–it was too bad. She was kind of nice. She was cute. I might have asked her out someday if I couldn't find the mysterious woman from the party. Then again, maybe it wouldn't be fair to her to come in second like that.

I caught up with Andrew, who had started to drive away before he spotted Emily and decided to watch us from afar. "Wanna go out?" he asked.

I wasn't sure what version of 'go out' he meant, but I agreed.

THE NEXT MORNING, I got out of bed with a full buzzing mind. It wasn't that I had any drinks when I went out with Andrew, but rather that I had a strange dream about the intriguing volunteer woman. I couldn't quite place the events, but I felt like in the dream we knew each other. Maybe it was because we got along so well and my mind was so desperate to find my mistletoe match. It was a fuzzy dream, like when you're looking through a frost-covered window. But I knew she had been there.

Too bad I would probably never be able to find her again either.

On top of the strange dream and the general grogginess I felt most mornings, as soon as I looked at my phone, I had about twelve more things making my mind buzz. Emily had sent me a message every forty five minutes since we parted the night before. I couldn't say that I was surprised. If anything, she was persistent when she wanted something. I just wished I wasn't on her radar anymore.

'I miss you.'

'Don't you miss me?'

'Is there someone else?'

'How could I ever love someone other than you?'

'Why won't you talk to me?'

'What did I do to make you hate me?'

'Let's try again.'

Now, my phone buzzed again. I saw that it was from her, but rather than reading it, I simply deleted it and tossed my phone onto my bed. I heard it buzz again.

This just wasn't going to end, not until I played a bit colder. I grabbed my phone from my twisted mess of sheets, brought up Emily's contact, and blocked her. I didn't feel the slightest tinge of guilt after I did it. I knew it was for the best. This was the official start of the official end.

I had a full day ahead of me and much more pressing things to think about. With the commencement of Christmas and the first of December over, there were a lot of calls for installing and wiring special Christmas displays and lights. That was probably eighty percent of my work in December. I didn't mind, though. I felt like I got to help fuel the town with the light and magic of Christmas.

I wondered what kind of thoughts my mystery match had about Christmas. I wondered what her name was, what she did for work, what she did for hobbies. I wondered where in Noel she lived. Or was she there at all? I was beginning to doubt that I'd actually seen her get in that van. Or maybe it was her friend's van or her friend worked at the bakery. Heck, maybe she'd stolen it for all I knew.

I rolled my eyes at myself. Even after being tricked by Emily for nearly two years in our relationship, I trusted myself not to pine over car thieves. I thought I had a better sense of character than that.

Then again, I had been, oh, so wrong about Emily. It still stung, if I was being honest, mostly because I was mad at myself for believing her con for so long. I wondered whether my mystery match would treat me the same way. I doubted it.

As crazy as it might have been to most people, I was totally taken in by her. She didn't have to do anything to hold my interest, except for the time we spent and our first kiss.

I pulled on a work polo and a pair of work jeans and looked at myself in the mirror. I tugged a dark blue hat on over my wild hair and gave myself a stern look in the eye. "I just know you'll find her," I told myself. Then I patted on some after-shave and headed off for work.

Throughout the day, I saw some postings for volunteer work and some other Christmas events around town. I thought it might be nice to run into the intriguing volunteer woman again if the chance occurred, but mostly I was holding out for the mistletoe woman. I figured if she attended the Santa Claus Ball, then maybe she would be at some of the other events in town. And maybe I should do some work or attend some events in Noel, too. That way, I could cover more bases.

When I got home from work and collapsed on the couch after a shower, I looked online and found a local toy drive event. It was in a couple of weeks, and I didn't want to wait that long. But I was willing to take every opportunity I could.

To make myself feel better, I also told myself that it was for the kids, not just to find my mystery woman. I enjoyed kids, and I really did want to support them. Christmas was always so important to me as a kid, so I wanted to make sure these other kids had some of those beautiful, uplifting experiences too.

Whether I found the girl or not, I decided it would be worth it to go, so I called to register.

CHAPTER 7

Holly

I WAS FEELING a lot of things. Between seeing the snow fall outside my window, my sweet little Carol setting her paw on my foot, and the oh-so-many thoughts hissing in my mind about the last week, I could not focus on my homework. Memories of the velvet-suited mystery man kissing me under the mistletoe kept popping up between every sentence in my Information Literacy assignment.

I had talked to both Abigail and Gretchen about it, because of course I had to. Gretchen kept asking if the mustache and beard combo had put a damper on it while Abigail was strangely silent about it. Yes, the mustache was there, and it may have been a little tickly on my top lip, but it didn't ruin the kiss, not in the slightest.

In fact, in my memories, there was no mustache. It was all floating candles and angels singing and fireworks exploding in the background. But, of course, that could have just been the adrenaline of making such a move.

Then, right alongside the little flits and airy tumbles my stomach was doing was the strange sense of guilt I felt because I had found another man attractive. And worse yet, I had even been a little disappointed that he wasn't single. And while I knew I didn't owe my mystery man anything just because of one magical kiss and a Christmas ball, it felt wrong to have my affections split.

Actually, it was probably for the best that this Patrick guy had a girlfriend because that meant he was off-limits. I didn't really need to think about him and his easy-going smile and his quippy, smart jokes. I really didn't need to think about the way his jeans fit his thighs or imagine what his arms and shoulders would look like.

I dropped my forehead into my arms and groaned. Carol looked up at me with a whine and pawed at my sweatpants.

"What do you think?" I asked her. "When you met the golden retriever at the park and the next week you met the Australian shepherd, how did you choose between them? And then when you found out that the golden retriever was about to have a litter with another dog, how did you get over that?"

I held a pencil to her like a microphone in a mock interview, but she just tried to eat it. I pulled it back quickly and pointed it at myself. "This is Holly Garland signing off before I have a mental breakdown from trying to get love advice from a dog."

What was I doing even thinking about getting hung up on a guy who had a girlfriend?

I stood up suddenly from my chair as if I'd had a eureka moment.

"I'm not going to!" I told myself. "You met the other guy first, and Patrick has a hot girlfriend anyway!"

Not to mention, that exceptional connection I'd had with velvet Mr. Claus in a span of two minutes, with minimal talking and never his seeing face. We weren't persuaded by outer appearances, though the velvet suit was an attention grabber. Still, that kind of closeness could rarely be felt in that kind of situation. Yet, it didn't feel like a flat, superficial link. It was more like an enchantment.

I couldn't let something like that go so easily.

Maybe I wasn't sure what to make of it all, but I wanted to find him regardless.

And the only way I could do that was if I continued to go out and went ahead with my lifelong love of Christmas, checking off all the things I wanted to do. Abigail had told me I needed to get back into my normal Christmas cheer, and she was right.

Carol looked up at me, giving tiny little woofs. She probably thought we were going for a walk. *And why let her down?*

I glanced outside and then looked down at my precious cairn terrier. She happened to love the snow just as much as I did, and we both needed a breath of that crisp, fresh winter air.

"Wanna go out?" I asked her.

She jumped up and turned in two circles before giving me a big, hearty bark. We walked to the front door, where I suited her up with her little winter vest and leash. The air outside had certainly gotten colder over the last week, but I welcomed the nip and the way it refreshed my senses. Carol seemed to enjoy it too because while she was generally good on the leash, she was pulling to get off the porch and into the snow.

We walked along the snow-covered sidewalk and Carol pounced through some of the snowdrifts. I liked hearing the crunch under my boots and seeing the tufts of white hanging onto the evergreen tree branches. This was part of the season so many people overlooked—the quiet, everyday beauty that it brought.

I enjoyed looking at people's decorations, too. And I spotted several new snowmen sculpted in yards down the block. I smiled to myself.

"It's time to whip out your Santa costume," I told Carol.

She didn't pay me any mind as she sniffed at the mailboxes decorated with holly and ribbons.

Shortly after arriving home and making myself a cup of hot cocoa loaded with marshmallows, I received a call from my mom.

"Hey!" I chirped.

My mom and I were always close growing up. Of course, I was fortunate to have a good relationship with both my parents, but the older I got, the more I felt like my mom and I were best friends. The more I could see myself in her, the more I was proud to be able to say that.

"Hey, cookie," she said. At one point I thought I'd outgrown that nickname, but eventually, I started to find it endearing. "What are you up to?"

"Carol and I just got back from a walk because I couldn't focus on my homework. I have this assignment to do about how to help users access information more easily and efficiently that I just cannot get into. Why do they assign all the boring stuff at the end of the semester when people are having a harder time focusing?"

My mom chuckled. "Well, every job has its boring parts. For instance, that's why I make your dad do all the financial stuff, and that's why I do all the baking stuff, but we both hate cleaning up."

"Isn't that what Jack is for?" I said jokingly.

"Well, yes, but I can't pawn those chores off on him forever or he'll never learn the business."

I knew she was right. But part of me didn't want him to learn the business because that would mean that my parents were giving it up. I knew that they deserved the extra time to relax and do things they hadn't made the time for over the last twenty-two years, but it was hard to accept that they were letting go of so many sentimental things, so many memories.

"Well, I know Jack will eventually take over, but why haven't you hired anyone to do the trivial things like run the register or wash the dishes?" I asked.

"Oh! Speaking of hiring people to help out," my mom said, ignoring my question. "What are you doing this weekend?"

"I don't have any plans set in stone yet," I explained.

"Well, if you're free, the church ladies and I are planning on going to the toy drive, but I'll admit I've fallen a bit behind on my end of the deal. Would you be willing to come help your poor old mom out?"

I chuckled. "You don't have to self-deprecate to guilt me into coming," I said. "I'm always willing to come help out. I love that place."

My mom let out the kind of hum that told me she was smiling but that she might feel a little sad or bittersweet about it. And for some reason, that made me feel less alone in my feelings about them handing off the bakery. Part of her probably felt a similar way.

"Anyway!" I said to break the growing silence. "You can sign me up. Maybe I'll even come for the weekend if Abigail is okay with hanging out with Carol."

"You don't want to bring Carol with you?" my mom asked.

Carol tended to get a little carsick if we drove longer than ten minutes. "I'll think about it," I said. "What time do you want me to come help you out?"

"Oh, I don't want to distract you from your schoolwork," she said. "I'd really just appreciate any time you could give me."

I wandered back to my room, blowing on my steaming hot chocolate and nabbing a slightly softened marshmallow between my lips. I used to eat all of the marshmallows right away so I could add more, but I'd gotten better at that over the years. I was a grown-up now.

I sucked up another mushy marshmallow.

Well, I was mostly grown up.

"Don't worry about the schoolwork. It's mostly final projects that we're working on all month. I have a lot of time to do them," I said. "How about I come the day before? That way, we have plenty of time?"

My mom hummed again, this time more hopefully. "Okay, if that's not a problem for you. Then let's plan on that. Really, you can come whenever you want."

My mom shared the details of the toy drive with me, when and what time. We chatted for a few more minutes about school and Christmas plans before she got interrupted by my dad needing assistance with a customer's order.

I tried to get back into my assignment, but my mind kept getting dragged away again. So instead of finishing my assignment, I researched the toy drive and read a couple of little news articles about it from the last few years. It was a nice charity that strived to give every child not only a suitable toy for Christmas, but they also supplied them and their family with all the food and home supplies they would need for the entire winter.

It seemed like it had become pretty big in the area, and even other cities donated items or funds to purchase the items. It was a noble cause that I was happy to be a part of. Before now, I'd been away at college, so I hadn't heard of it.

While I was searching, I saw several opportunities for charities, and the Christmas spirit moved me to join. In the middle of rearranging my whole calendar for the month of December, Abigail arrived home from her job and became a victim of my planning. I talked her into going to a few events with me, and she made me schedule some "fun" things too.

But it was all fun—it was Christmas, after all.

With my mind and my heart felt overjoyed with my new plans, I almost forgot about my mystery man.

Almost.

But between Abigail nagging me and getting a reminder from my professor about the due date of the assignment as well as a pop quiz the next day, I figured that the rest of the night needed to be spent with my fingers on the keyboard or my nose in a textbook.

I forced myself back into studying while sugarplums danced in the back of my mind.

CHAPTER 8

Patrick

BRIGHT AND EARLY ON Saturday morning, I drove to Noel to help out in the toy drive, hoping I'd get to see my Mistletoe Mystery woman.

It actually wasn't the first time I had volunteered at this particular event. A few years prior, I had come here with Emily. At the time, I felt happy about her willingness to help children. But I'd taken off my rose-colored glasses since then, and looking back, it seemed more likely she just wanted to have five minutes of fame on the one-off television show that was covering the event.

She'd only been there long enough to hold a kid in her lap while they asked her questions about volunteering and helping the needy. She'd spewed some lies about how she always adored kids and couldn't wait to be a mother one day. She said she wished she were a bit older so she could consider adopting. Looking back, she only ever talked about herself. She didn't even mention the kid, not even the one sitting on her lap. It was like that poor little five-year-old boy was just a prop to make her look more saintly.

Thinking about that, I started feeling guilty about the reason I was going there. This was about helping those in need, assisting families that couldn't afford a holiday dinner much less presents for all of their kids. Because of the stitch of guilt I'd sewn into the back of my mind, I skipped the coffee I was going to grab and made sure I arrived early.

For a moment, I worried whether Emily would show up, but when I learned that only the regular news channel would be there for a few minutes to promote the event, I figured I was safe from another unexpected visit.

When I arrived, there were already a few families lined up for help. With most of them, I would have never guessed that they were struggling. Then there were some other families that were a little more obviously down on their luck. The children had worn sneakers and the slightly greasy hair, the little discoloration under their eyes from being under-nourished.

"Where do you want me?" I asked as I signed in.

A middle-aged woman carrying a clipboard flipped through some papers. "There's nobody stationed at the toy table. How about that?" she asked. Then she lifted the board to cover half her face and leaned in as if to tell me a secret. "That's the best seat in the house."

I laughed. "Because it's the most fun?" I whispered back.

She smiled at me. "It's fun. You get the most laughs and smiles. And it's next to the cookie table."

I glanced across the room. A couple of older folks were walking around, pulling a tablecloth over a couple of tables. "Is it the best? Or is it the most torturous?"

The woman with the clipboard shrugged. "Depends on how nice you are to the cookie people."

I parted ways with the clipboard woman and began to examine my station. There was a system for the toys split between boys and girls. I wasn't the kind of guy to assume that all boys wanted trucks while all girls wanted Barbies. But while I was making a new organization system, someone came by and told me not to change too much. I complied, but decided that it would still be best to let the kids choose whatever they wanted.

A young man with a clipboard and a name badge reading "Ty" came by shortly after that and told me I'd likely have one or two helpers, and then someone would come to relieve me for a lunch break.

As I continued to settle in, I spotted the cookie people loading up their tables. The older man and woman looked familiar, but I couldn't quite place them. After all, I'd been all over Noel for the last couple of weeks. I scanned the room, which was growing busier and busier, wondering what the likelihood of finding my match would be. Then I glanced outside at the families and reorganized my priorities–the doors would be opening soon.

Just a couple of minutes before the church opened the door, my helper arrived. He was a high-school aged kid with curly red hair and green Converse. His name was Oliver. We didn't have much time to become acquainted and come up with a strategy before the toy drive officially got started.

I loved that I had come to support this cause because it was so much more than just a toy drive. Families received new clothes, food, and household items, and they got to top it off with special gifts like toys for their kids and sweet treats. Lots of people showed up and just five minutes in, I was in the zone.

I had forgotten how much I enjoyed kids. Their joy and inno-cence was heartwarming and it gave me hope for the world. Most of the kids were grateful to receive anything, and a few of them even cried at getting to choose their own toy. I was glad that I had done this, no matter what the original intention had been. Giving out toys alone probably touched the hearts of these kids, but I was here helping do more than that. Every high five and fist bump and hug these children got was a connection, a reminder that someone had their back and someone cared about them, that someone saw them.

One little girl, probably about seven years old, nearly brought me to tears when she thanked me for the gift and immediately turned around and gave the toy to her older sister, who was probably twelve. "I wanted to give this to you," she told her sister, "because you don't have a doll. Now we can play together!" The mom watched with a bittersweet expression that I couldn't even begin to understand.

I gave the little girl another doll, and she looked so happy. As they walked away, I turned to avoid anyone seeing me shed a tear—it just seemed unprofessional. I didn't want to ruin the mood. But to my surprise, I met eyes with someone familiar.

She was apparently volunteering too, except she was stationed a couple tables over at the home supplies booth. When she caught my gaze, she smiled and waved. It was a cute, shy smile that brought a little bit of pinkness to her cheeks. I was surprised to see her—Holly. How could I have forgotten a classic Christmas name like that? I grinned and smiled back.

Eventually, when we caught a lull and another volunteer had arrived to give me a break, I left the table for a moment to go say hi. She spotted me making my way over and pardoned herself as well. We found ourselves meeting in the middle at the big Christmas tree with blue and silver ribbons cascading from the top to the floor.

"Holly!" I said, maybe a bit too cheerfully. I really wasn't expecting to see her there.

"Patrick," she said back, a bit awkwardly as she clenched her hands together in front of her.

I was happy that she remembered my name.

"I'm surprised to see you. I assumed you lived in Mistletoe Mountain," I said.

She nodded. "I do. I'm just here visiting and volunteering. I thought *you* lived in Mistletoe Mountain."

I laughed. "Oh. I do. I guess I just didn't expect to run into another commuter."

She grinned, and a short silence grew between us as we both hesitated to say something.

"So, how are things going with the toys?" she finally asked.

I felt a bit ridiculous that I had suddenly forgotten how to carry a conversation, but I was grateful for her ice-breaking skills. "It's so great getting to see some of these kids get to accept a Christmas present. I can't imagine what it means to them. It seems like such a small gesture, but I'm sure they'll grow up being able to appreciate Christmas and experience that good old holiday cheer."

Holly smiled. I noticed the slightest dimple in her cheek. "Aww, that's cute," she said. "I'm jealous. I know it's important, but handing out toilet paper doesn't give a lot of people the glittery, fluttery feelings."

"Aw, come on," I said. "Don't sell your role short. What will people appreciate more when they're in the bathroom–toilet paper or a superhero action figure that punches?"

She crossed her arms casually and shrugged. "Depends on how bored you are, I guess."

I chuckled. I remembered that she had been quite funny that night when I first met her.

"But how do I know you're doing the job well?" she asked, narrowing her eyes at me. "Are you capable of matching the right toy with the right kid?"

"Hah!" I guffawed playfully. "Of course. I'm the best man for the job!"

"The best man?" she asked with uncertainty.

I nodded with confidence. "I'm a professional when it comes to toys."

Holly raised an eyebrow. "Professional with toys?"

"I'm practically a ten-year-old boy at heart," I boasted as if that were something someone in their early twenties should be proud about. "I know it all."

"Even the girl stuff?" she challenged me.

I scoffed. "You know how Beach Ken is good at 'beach?' Well, Patrick," I gestured to myself with my thumbs, "is good at toys."

"Ken as in Barbie's Ken?" she asked.

I nodded again.

Holly just blinked at me for a moment before breaking into a smile. "Alright. Well, I think I don't have the choice but to believe you. But you best know that I'll be keeping an eye on you from over there," she said, pointing back to her station, "to make sure you're doing a sufficient job."

Something lifted in my stomach, like I'd just dropped over a hill at high speed. I liked the idea of her keeping an eye on me. I felt a slow grin lift on one side. "Alright. I look forward to that."

Holly glanced over her shoulder. "I think I better get back," she said.

I nodded. "Me too," I said. As she turned to leave, I stopped her. "Holly!"

She paused and looked back at me.

"If you need any help, I also know a lot about toilet paper!"

She rolled her eyes and smirked before turning around.

After we parted ways, I got swept up into my work, unless you count the few times I glanced up to see if Holly was indeed keeping an eye on me. I found myself feeling a little let down when I didn't meet her eyes once. I supposed I was feeling hopeful that she might like me.

A little while past noon, I was relieved for an hour lunch break. When I made it to the little break room, to my sweet surprise, Holly was seated at one of the round tables, snacking on a triangle half of a sandwich.

"Hey!" I said. "You're here too."

She swallowed her bite and nodded. "I am indeed." Then she nodded toward the counter behind her. "Free lunch. Pick a sandwich, some chips and cookies, and a drink."

I followed her suggestion and sat beside her. I hoped it wasn't too presumptuous and that she was okay with me doing so. "You seem like a pro," I told her. "Do you come here for this every year?"

"Oh, the 'Professional with Toys' is calling *me* a pro? I'm flattered!" she said, pressing her hand to her chest with faux honor.

I knocked her elbow playfully with mine and popped open my bag of kettle cooked chips.

"Nah, I've been here a lot in my youth, but as an adult only a couple of times. My parents do it every year. How about you?"

I cracked open my soda can. "A while back I came with my girlfriend, but this is only my second time."

"Oh, is your girlfriend here, too?" Holly asked. Then she immediately took another bite of her sandwich.

I kicked myself for referring to Emily as my girlfriend, but I supposed it was an old habit. She was the only girlfriend I'd ever had. "Ah, no." I said, waving my hand. Then wanting to ensure I was clear, I added, "We broke up. It's been over a year now. I don't have a girlfriend."

Holly hummed indifferently as she continued to chew her bite of sandwich.

"What about you? Boyfriend? Is he around—"

She shook her hand. "Don't have one," she said.

"Oh," I said, trying to match her indifference.

"I've been focused on school. Even the poor jerk I dated in high school wouldn't qualify as a boyfriend because I was so wrapped up in AP classes," she explained. "When I got to college, I just kept my eye on the prize."

I found myself wanting to know more about her, wanting to keep the conversation going, not just for conversation sake but because I liked to hear her talk.

"What's the prize?" I asked.

She shrugged. "Graduation, I guess. I never wanted to stay in school for long, so I did everything I could to ensure I'd be done early."

We got into talking about school and she explained that she had double-majored in English Literature and Library Science and that she wanted to be a librarian.

"Actually, this whole last week I've been working on finals. They're supposed to post our final grades around 1:00 today."

I glanced down at my watch and grinned. I showed it to her. "Would you look at that?"

She gulped down another bite. "Oh," she said, looking a little nervous.

"Do you want to check?" I asked her.

She hesitated. "Is it weird that I'm scared?"

"Why would you be scared?" I asked, resting my arm on the table.

Holly set down her sandwich and leaned back in her chair, fiddling with the hem of her sweater. "If I pass, then I've graduated. I mean, I've always been a good student, so I'm sure I'm good, but... I don't know if I'm one-hundred percent ready to move on to the next thing."

I couldn't help but sympathize. "Well, it might not make you feel better, but we're rarely one hundred percent ready for anything," I told her.

She looked at me, right in the eyes. Heck, maybe so deep she was staring into my soul. Maybe this was the first time I'd really looked at her. Her eyes were a beautiful earthy green color that had seemed brown until now.

"Let's check it out," I encouraged her.

She took in and let out a big sigh before taking her phone out. She was silent as she thumbed her screen. And then... a slow, sneaky smile spread across her face.

"You did it," I said in a quiet voice.

She glanced at me and her smile grew a bit wider. There was that peek of a dimple again. "I'm done," she said.

"Well! This deserves a celebration!" I cheered. "Are you going to party it up?"

She looked at me doubtfully. "How many librarians do you know who like to 'party it up'?"

I shrugged. "Well as the Professional with Toys, I'm also pretty much the Professional of All Things Fun. I can plan a wide variety of parties."

"Do you have a 'congratulations on becoming an adult, I hope you don't fail' party plan?" she asked, setting her phone face-down on the table.

I crossed my arms coolly. "I have some ideas. Just leave it to me."

"You're really gonna plan my graduation party?" she asked, bewildered. "You don't even know me."

It might have seemed strange, but I did want to do something for her. Call it the Christmas spirit, but I just wanted to spread some of this cheer.

"If you're down with it," I said, leaning forward to rest my elbows on the table. I was honestly feeling a little worried that she might think I was a weirdo and turn down my idea, especially the longer she was quiet.

Then she hummed and just said, "Okay. Let's do it. You can plan a party for me."

CHAPTER 9

Holly

THE DAY STARTED WITH A DREAM.

I was standing in front of the biggest Christmas tree in town, the one in the center of the square, right outside the city courthouse. It looked a lot like the tree from the Santa Claus Ball. It was decorated with the same giant intricate Christmas balls, silver tinsel, and beautiful vintage ornaments. Red bows were tied all over it, and a giant crystal star shone at the top of the tree.

This time, the mistletoe seemed to be floating in the sky. I was admiring it, and it began to snow. The snow was almost blue, and it sparkled as if enshrouded in magic. Then, something caused me to turn around. I came face-to-face with a man dressed in a red velvet suit, but his face was covered with a mask. When he spoke there was no sound, but I felt my heart begin to race as he leaned in toward me and gently placed a hand on my cheek. Just like that night, I rose up on my tiptoes and met the mystery man's lips.

I recalled the way I got so lost in it that it felt like I was floating up into the sky, like I should be up there twirling around with the bright mistletoe. His lips were warm and soft but he kissed me with a certain depth that I could only describe as spellbinding. But when he pulled away and I opened my eyes, he wasn't there, and the whole space around me had gone gray-black.

I awoke suddenly, not with a jerk like you see in the movies, but when my eyes popped open I was just as awake as if I'd never fallen asleep in the first place. I got out of bed in a daze. The dream made me feel like that kiss was just moments before, like it had happened for the first time all over again.

So when I got the reminder on my phone that today was the day Patrick was taking me out for a graduation celebration, I felt a bit strange. I couldn't forget the sensation of that kiss under the mistletoe. Yet, I was excited to go on a date with this other cute guy who'd I'd now run into two times. I wished I knew who the other guy was so I could track him down and find out if our attraction stretched farther than that night and those few minutes we got to dance together, farther than that magical moment our lips met.

All through the day, my dream haunted me. I spent a few hours in the early afternoon working at the bookstore, and it lingered there in the back of my mind. It was a slow day for a Friday in December, but I thought maybe people were waiting for our best promotion the week before Christmas. That meant there was hardly anything to keep me from thinking about it. I got to scan books to mark down for the clearance sale, but that was a rather mindless job.

I was feeling a little ragged by the time I made it home. Carol greeted me with her stubby wagging tail and her moist nose. Even on our walk that afternoon, my thoughts drifted like the snow, lazy and beautiful and cold. Aside from the memory of the kiss, the velveted-suited mystery man seemed so far away. I had had no leads for finding him—though I hadn't really been trying my best other than scanning crowds more purposefully and trying to meet more gazes.

What more could I have done?

But the truth of the matter was, I didn't know anything about that man. But based on his confidence and his suit alone, I thought he might be some well-off guy who I wouldn't have stood the chance of meeting any other way.

When Abigail got home, she noticed right away I seemed trapped in my mind. She was insightful like that. And she was honest enough to tell me rather than being gentle about it.

"What's got you locked up in your prison mind this time?" she asked.

I shrugged. "I know it's nearing two weeks away, but I had this strange dream last night about the guy from the Santa Claus Ball… and now I can't seem to get him off my mind."

Abigail plopped down on the couch and embraced one of the fluffy white throw pillows. "Aren't you going on that date tonight with that Patrick guy?" she asked.

My heart ached a bit. "Patrick is a good guy, but I started having feelings for the velvet-suited man before I'd ever met him. Granted, I actually know Patrick and I have a good time with him."

"In my opinion," Abigail said, "I think it's best to pursue what you can feel. There's this whole thing about chasing your dreams that I never quite understood. Like, it's invisible. It's not guaranteed. You never know what's going to happen, so why take an unnecessary chance when you have a more secure thing in front of you?"

I knew what she meant, but I was also sure that she'd never experienced something like I had. She was too cut and dry for that, not that it was a bad thing.

"Anyway, I'm not saying you have to commit yourself to Patrick," she went on. "I'm simply suggesting that if you like him, put more time into getting to know him and don't spend too much time pondering over 'what ifs' like you can change them."

She was right. I had to admit it. Maybe I was clinging a little too tightly to this magical fairytale image. I really was excited to see what Patrick had in store for my celebration, so I told myself I was going to focus on having a good night. I had no idea what he might have planned, and part of me hoped that it was nothing too extravagant.

"I'm going to get ready," I said, standing.

Abigail smiled and stood up with me. "I have the perfect outfit for you to wear."

PATRICK WAS DRESSED HANDSOMELY in a gray-blue sweater that matched his eyes. The collar from his button down shirt underneath was popped out neatly. His sandy brown hair was combed nicely, and I liked that he left it to curl naturally at the ends. I could tell he was freshly shaven, and he smelled fresh, woodsy, and warm with hints of geranium and cedarwood.

"You look nice," he told me.

I had let him pick me up at my house. My car had been fixed, so I was willing to meet him somewhere, but he had insisted, so I agreed.

"Like, really nice," he added.

I stifled a little giggle that felt very much unlike myself. But I had to admit that I felt good about the outfit Abigail had loaned me, and she'd helped with my hair and light makeup. I was flattered that he felt that way. I smiled and gestured to myself. "Why, thank you."

He opened the door of his pickup for me and I climbed in. When he settled himself in the driver's seat, I glanced over at him and let myself study him for a moment. "You look really nice, too," I said.

He stopped turning the key and looked through the little curl of bangs that nearly covered his eyes. He gave me half a grin. "I'm glad you think so."

I tried to find out where we were headed, but he asked me to trust him. And I did. It was only the third time I'd met him, and it was the first time we were alone together, but I truly felt safe with Patrick.

About ten minutes later, we arrived at a nice restaurant. I'd seen it in passing, heard about it on social media. It was a small but rather fancy looking joint with lots of twinkle light ambience. There was light chatter, but it was altogether quiet and intimate. We were sitting off to the side at a private table with only two seats and a small, golden candle holder supporting two twisted lit candles.

"Did you make a reservation?" I asked Patrick.

He shrugged as he sat down in front of me. "Yes, I planned it. You said I could, remember?"

It was true, and I nodded. This was both more and less than I was expecting. I was beginning to think he had asked me out under the guise of a graduation party because this was totally a date setting. But I decided not to read too much into it. I'd told him that he could plan and I'd given no guidelines, so it was only fair of me to wait it out and see what else was going to happen.

"So, Holly Garland," Patrick said, twisting his fingers around his glass. "Tell me about yourself."

I lightly rolled my eyes. "Is that the best you got?" I asked. "That's the default. That's what everyone says."

He smirked at me and looked off to the side as if searching for inspiration for a different question. "Touché. Then... tell me about the very first Christmas you remember."

I smiled. "Actually, nobody would ever believe me, but I think I remember my first Christmas," I said. I almost expected Patrick to laugh at me or look doubtful, but he just gleamed at me with expectant eyes and an intrigued expression. So, I continued. "It's nothing crazy. But I remember feeling warm. I remember slow-blinking colorful lights. I remember feeling... safe."

I knew logically, it probably wasn't believable. As a nearly two-month-old baby, I probably wouldn't have been capable of knowing what safety was, so I probably didn't feel it.

"That's beautiful," Patrick said. "You've got a true Christmas spirit in you, I think."

The way he was looking at me was nice, but I was starting to become too aware of myself. "What about you?"

Patrick thought for a moment before speaking. "I think I was five. I remember my dad holding me up so I could turn on the light on top of the tree. I remember wearing these little footy pajamas with reindeer on them. It had a little hood with antlers and everything."

I smiled as I listened to him. His voice was soothing. The way he spoke made me feel like I was listening to a sweet bedtime story.

"My dad and I would sneak into the kitchen and eat too many

cookies. I'm sure now my mom knew what was going on, but she would always feign ignorance. I remember watching some old black-and-white show, but I can't recall what it might have been. And my mom wrapped an extra scarf around me before my dad and I went outside to play in the snow. Now that I'm thinking of it, every Christmas felt like that, like a rerun that never got old."

I wanted to reach across the table and touch Patrick's hand because he started to speak with sadness. But I didn't. We talked about Christmas for a while before we started speaking of school, and I learned more about his business as an electrician. I was kind of surprised that was his chosen profession, but I supposed I didn't know him that well just yet.

When it came time for dessert, Patrick rose from the table and excused himself for a minute. He came back wearing a big grin and wiggling his eyebrows. I wondered just what he had up his sleeve.

"Can you stand up for a moment?" he asked.

I looked around the small restaurant before scooting my chair back and standing. Patrick approached me with his hands behind his back. My heart began to race. It felt like a movie scene, like the kind where the guy proposes....

Suddenly, Patrick wrapped something around me, sliding a big black satin loop over my head, and lifting one of my arms to put outside of it. I stared at him with confusion.

He just chuckled and said to take a look.

I glanced down and lifted the black satin sash. In scrawling silver letters it read, 'graduate.' My heart crashed with relief and my face settled back into an easy smile. "Where did you find this on such short notice?" I asked.

He ignored my question and took something else out from behind his back and placed it on my head. I reached up to touch it. It was smooth and square-shaped with something dangling down in front.

"Is this a–" I began.

Patrick cut me off gently with a nod and gestured for me to sit down. But he didn't sit. I thought that was suspicious too. But then I heard it... coming from somewhere back in the kitchen was a familiar song, except they'd changed the words to sing 'congratulations to you' instead of 'happy birthday to you" as the staff carried out a single chocolate cupcake with little drops of confetti icing. It was topped with a cute little fondant graduation cap and a single, lit candle.

Pretty soon the eyes of everyone in the restaurant were on me, and it seemed like most of them were singing along, too. It was surprising and embarrassing and adorable all at once. My parents were great and supportive and always celebrated me, but I'd never experienced anything quite like this before. It did make me feel a bit special and rosy.

I found myself standing to receive the cupcake as if it were my diploma. Patrick patted me gently on the back, his hand warm and comforting. I met his eyes, and they were glittering with excitement, maybe pride.

Why on earth would this near stranger feel so proud of me? Regardless, it felt nice.

"You gotta move the tassel!" some older man from across the restaurant yelled.

"May I?" Patrick asked since my hands were full with the cupcake.

I nodded and stood still to let him reach up. He reached up and gently moved the red tassel from one side to the other. Then he started a big round of applause, and the entire restaurant joined in.

I felt my cheeks warm with embarrassment, but I was happy. And I felt proud of myself, too.

Patrick and I enjoyed our desert, but I asked to keep my cupcake for a couple more days before I decided to eat it. Just when we got back to his truck and I thought he was going to take me home, he asked if I was up for a movie.

"You choose," he said. "They're showing *It's a Wonderful Life* and *Miracle on 34th Street.*"

"What an impossible decision," I said. "They're both classics!"

Patrick chuckled and pointed the vents toward me to lend me more heat. I'd barely noticed myself that I was bouncing my legs from the cold.

"Well," he said. "On one hand, you've got a story about family and love and innocence and coming together as a community and believing, but on the other hand, you've got joy and laughter and finding meaning in life."

I raised an eyebrow. "You know these movies yourself or did you just google them?"

Patrick laughed aloud but didn't answer. He was becoming a mystery tonight. Every time he did something unexpected, I found myself wanting to know more about him.

"Why don't you choose?" I said.

He gave a quick upside down smile. "Very well."

We rode in comfortable silence to the movie theater, just listening to the jingle of old-timey Christmas carols. When he finally arrived at the theater, Patrick came around and opened the door for me. He paid for my ticket but didn't tell me what movie it was for. And as we walked through the dim-lit theater, he guided me gently with a hand on my back.

This really was feeling more and more like a date.

But as we watched *Miracle of 34th Street*, he never made any moves, and he was the perfect gentleman. I was a bit bewildered, a bit let down, and a bit eased of the pressure I thought I had been placing on myself as I wondered whether this was a date or not.

Patrick was great. He was thoughtful, kind and funny. He was confident and easy-going, and... maybe unavailable, I thought as we exited the movie theater.

The thought came because I spotted that same woman who'd visited him after the volunteer day in the park. She was standing by the door in a nice black cape with fur lining the hood. Her arms were crossed, and her bright red lips were twisted in a disapproving grimace. She looked like a sassy Snow White.

I paid her no mind and walked to Patrick's truck.

CHAPTER 10

Patrick

I WASN'T sure whether or not I wanted to admit that our outing was a date, but the longer we were together, the more it felt like it. I had found Holly especially beautiful tonight with her long auburn hair curled and her green eyes shining brightly with surprise. She had worn such a cute expression when I put the sash over her head and set the grad cap gently atop her hair.

And when she thought that was all but the whole restaurant starting singing to her, the pink color of her cheeks alone warmed me, though the smile she wore really tugged at my heartstrings. I wondered if something else like this had ever been done for her before.

When we talked about Christmas and shared some of our favorite memories, I felt like we could talk forever. And when we rode in the truck to the movie in silence, I wasn't uncomfortable. I didn't feel the pressure to keep up the conversation like I had felt in other situations. I hadn't really known my intentions when I asked her if I could plan this, but it was becoming clearer the more I spent time with her.

I was starting to have feelings for her.

But was it wrong of me to harbor feelings for her when that kiss under the mistletoe with another woman had been weighing so heavily on my mind? I wondered if I should move forward with Holly when my mystery match had already caught my attention and affection.

I wasn't sure if I was any closer to finding her, so that made me think that it was okay for me to go out with Holly again. Then again, when little things Holly did reminded me of my mystery match, I felt a little guilty that I was thinking of someone else.

As much as I loved to see Holly laugh, every time she did it shook something loose in me. If only I'd met Holly that night. Maybe I wouldn't have been so torn.

I wrestled with those thoughts as I worked through the morning. Things were starting to pick up at work as some people were discovering that they needed to update their wiring or needed inspections. I arrived at my one o'clock appointment, and just as I'd gotten out of the truck to grab my things, a familiar black Challenger pulled in behind me.

I gritted my teeth and tried to brace myself for what was to come.

Emily got out of her car and all but slammed the door. She marched up to me and stopped nearly toe-to-toe.

"What are you doing here?" I asked. "How did you know where I was going to be?"

She crossed her arms and grimaced. She was playing it tough today, by her expression. I wondered what she was so upset about this time.

"You have a new girlfriend already?" she said accusingly.

I rubbed my face with my hands. "This is ridiculous."

"How can you do that?" she said through her teeth.

"Emily," I said, attempting to step around her. "It's one thing for you to follow me to work, and I'm willing to overlook that for now. However, since I *am* at my place of work, can you please not do this now?"

She shuffled behind me in her kitten-heeled booties and grabbed my arm. "Would you just answer me?" she demanded. "What was that whole cheesy, romantic scene in the restaurant? Are you dating her?"

How did she know about that? She had to have followed us. Truly, her obsession with getting back together was going too far now.

I slowly turned around to face her and looked her in the face. Her skin had lost its color. It seemed paler than usual. "It's none of your business, Emily. Like I said before, you need to go."

"You didn't even answer my question!" she said, raising her voice.

"Because you don't need to know!" I yelled back at her. I caught myself and clasped my hands together tightly. I recomposed myself. "Please, for your sake and for mine, forget about me and move on. That's what I'm trying to do."

She pinched her eyebrows together tightly and looked me in the eyes fiercely. "I can't believe you," she muttered. "Fine, if you think you're going to move on, then I guess I have no choice."

I turned back to my truck to retrieve my tools. Emily seemed to finally get the hint that I wasn't going to engage with her anymore. She left in a huff. I hoped this would be the last instance and she would just leave me alone now.

After I finished my one o'clock job, I had to buy supplies for some lighting installations planned throughout the week. Then, toward the end of the day, I carved out time for Mrs. Henson. I had felt bad that I hadn't seen her as often since I was so preoccupied trying to find my mystery woman.

Around four o'clock, I stopped by her house for a surprise visit. She answered the door wrapped up in a shawl like usual with her feet tucked into a pair of fuzzy slippers.

"Patrick!" she said with delight. "Why, what are you doing here?"

She stepped through the door to give me a hug and then pulled me inside. "I just wanted to see you," I told her.

Mrs. Henson chuckled and waved me over. "Or someone paid you to come check on me."

"The payment was extra. I was coming to see you anyway," I told her with a wink.

She scrunched her nose at me and turned around to pour some coffee in a vintage looking mug with little yellow flowers painted on the side. "Cream or sugar?"

"Cream, please." I sat down at her little round table and pulled out a little gift I had bought her. One day last week, while I was out and about traipsing through the Christmas stores, I spotted a beautiful white ceramic cross that I thought she might like to hang on her tree. I'd gotten a small box from the store and wrapped the present with a little ribbon.

She turned to set down the mug in front of me and she spotted the little box on the table. "What's this?" she asked, picking it up to inspect it.

"It's just a little something I picked up for you," I told her.

She seemed genuinely surprised. "A gift for me? Why, we've still got more than two weeks until Christmas."

I shrugged and helped her to untie the ribbon when she started trying to untie it but her fingers were no longer nimble enough to grip the little strings. "I can't wait until Christmas. I want you to see it and use it now."

She laid down the ribbon on the table and gingerly lifted off the lid of the box. Her face fell into an upside down smile as she looked at the gift. "Oh, Patrick," she said softly. "This is just so beautiful. Thank you so much."

"I thought you might like to put it on your tree," I said, smiling.

Mrs. Henson hesitated. "Oh, well," she glanced behind her toward the living room.

I looked too. "You're not telling me…." I got up and walked to the living room. "Grace! How could you not have your tree up yet?"

I should have noticed that the last time I'd been there.

"Where is your tree?" I asked her.

She looked down sadly. "It's still in the attic, I'm afraid. I can't get up there anymore."

"You should have told me!" I said, trying not to sound upset. "Or I'm sure my aunt would have helped you."

Mrs. Henson shrugged. "I already ask so much of you two. I don't want you to feel like you have to do every little thing for me."

I walked over to her and wrapped an arm over her narrow, thin shoulders. "Tell me this. Do you want your tree up?" I asked.

She hesitated to respond but eventually nodded her head.

"Well, I, for one, love decorating trees," I told her. "A lot of people might think it's for women or for kids or whatever, but there's something soothing in it. It just makes me feel lighter, happier."

Mrs. Henson looked up at me with a small smile. "I like the way the colorful lights shine on the wall, and when you're outside you can see them glowing behind the window."

"Then it sounds like we better get this thing up!" I declared.

She agreed and let me help her set up her tree. She told me how she and her husband used to decorate it the Sunday after Thanksgiving, but this year she hadn't wanted to do it alone. It would have made her feel too sad. My heart ached for her, and I made a mental note to visit her on Christmas. Or maybe I'd see if my aunt would invite her to a gathering.

We worked slowly on the tree, and I did most of the organizing of the branches since Mrs. Henson said she couldn't see the worn-out painted colors on the metal hooks of the branches. We strung the lights together, reaching our arms around the tree to pass the string of lights to each other. And I took on the job of unwrapping the newspaper from the ornaments while she placed them carefully on the tree.

The final touches were to place the star on top, which she asked me to please do. And then she chose a place right at the front to hang the little white cross that I'd bought for her. We admired our handy work after plugging the lights in.

"How about some old Christmas tunes?" she asked.

I smiled. "Bring it on!"

Mrs. Henson pulled out a few old Christmas records and placed them on the turntable, twisting the volume up so that the light, cheery tune slowly filled the house. She stood and looked at the tree with a peaceful expression. It was a little melancholy, but there was a hint of a smile there that told me she was going to be okay. She just needed some quiet time.

It was just in time to give her some space, because my phone began to vibrate in my pocket. For a moment I worried that it might be Emily, but I remembered that I had blocked her number. When I saw the name, my chest filled with eager anticipation.

"Holly?" I said as I answered.

"Hi, Patrick," she responded. "Sorry for calling you out of the blue, but I had a proposal for you."

My heart was pounding. We'd texted a few times since our 'date,' but this was the first time she'd ever called me. It was surreal hearing her voice on the other end of the line. I tried to keep my cool. "And what might that be?"

"Well," she began slowly, "you like volunteering…."

"Yes."

"And you like kids…."

"Yes," I said again.

"Am I'm inclined to believe that you like sugar and creating things since you're the Professional of Fun, was it?"

I wondered where this was going, but I was intrigued, and I felt like I was going to agree no matter what this proposal entailed. "Professional with Toys, but go on."

She stifled a cute laugh before she continued. "Anyway, maybe you already have plans…."

"It seems like you knew everything about me, but not this thing?" I interrupted.

"Oh, hush," she said, laughing. "Do you have plans this weekend or not?"

I couldn't contain my smile. "Not."

I sensed an eye roll, and that made my smile even harder to control. "Well, since you're not busy, would you want to do something with me? It involves all aforementioned things, specifically, the sweet things are gingerbread houses."

"Of course I'll do that with you," I said.

Holly was too quiet for a short moment. "Great, then you'll pick me up?"

"Yes, my lady. Anything for you, my lady," I teased.

When I hung up the phone Mrs. Henson was sipping her coffee and staring at me with a knowing smile.

"You got a new girlfriend?" she asked.

CHAPTER 11

Holly

Now that we were just two weeks from Christmas, the bookstore was getting crazy busy. And since I was done with school, I had started working longer hours. But it would be short lived. I had planned to make it through the holiday season with my bookstore job. I wasn't rude enough to quit at peak busy season. But I'd just gotten confirmation this morning that I'd been accepted for a position as a teacher's aide that I would start at the beginning of the year, after Christmas vacation was over.

It was only a few weeks away. When I applied for that job one of those restless nights a couple weeks ago, I didn't think they'd take me. I was too fresh out of college, and I was only twenty-one. But I supposed my parents had taught me to be responsible since I was young and I'd been so dedicated to my studies that I never got in the habit of nonsense, so that probably made me seem more mature to most people.

Now, I was excited for it. I had something to look forward to. Really, I was growing a bit tired of school and work. I was ready to *do* something, and after helping out at some of the volunteer events over the last couple of weeks, I was starting to think I'd really like to work with kids. So far I'd been so interested in books, character growth, building worlds with words, and creating plot lines that rose and fell all at the right times. I wanted to understand that and work in an environment where I could help people find books that suited them, but now I was thinking I wanted a little more than that.

I'd keep my job at the bookstore and go back to part-time evenings and probably hop on some weekends, but I was ready to do something different. I liked the work at the bookstore, and I liked reading, but perhaps I was going to like working with kids more.

Between scanning books and helping customers find gifts for their kids and their loved ones and friends, I wondered how I'd fit into a classroom. I always imagined myself somewhere a little more solitary. I liked being around people, but I had always really loved the library and books. It had only made sense for my goal to be working in a library. And the library that I had gone to as a child always had fun events with themes and prizes and getting to meet other kids. I wanted to be a part of that. Now, instead, I would be in a school, where kids were bouncing off the walls and crying and causing trouble. I hoped that I could handle it.

I smiled to myself, imagining what the classrooms might be like, what kids would take a liking to me, who would test me in the beginning just to become the favorite.

I packed up my customers' books and slid in a coupon for their next visit. They said a quick thank you and scurried away, probably to buy more gifts.

It seemed like I had caught a break in customers, and I was really starting to feel exhausted. I hadn't gotten to take my lunch yet due to the sudden spike in visitors. I turned to find the schedule that told me which employee would relieve me of my duties at the register. As I was scanning the list, I sensed someone approaching the register.

"Hey," someone said briskly.

In my mind I prepared myself to deal with a difficult customer. We always had them. It was inevitable. Not everyone in the world was kind, patient, and understanding. Some people had no regard for others, and by the tone of this lady's voice, she wasn't one to take it easy on anyone.

I turned around swiftly and put on my best customer service smile and voice. "Hello, how can I help you today?" I asked.

But upon turning around I found a familiar face, one that made the pits of my stomach churn with discomfort.

It was her, the girlfriend–Patrick's. He hadn't mentioned much about her other than explaining that they had broken up over a year ago and she was occasionally showing back up into his life to bug him about it. He hadn't told me why they broke up, just that she wasn't the kind of person he thought she was. When she started showing her true colors, he got out.

"What do you think you're doing?" she growled at me.

This girl was scary. The look in her eyes was like that of a wild cougar defending its territory. I was glad that I had the service counter between us. Her long, straight black hair dangled over her shoulder as she leaned toward me.

"Sorry, I was just checking the schedule," I said nicely. "What can I do for you?"

"Oh, you want to help me?" she said with a sarcastic smile. "Great! Then you can stay away from Patrick."

My customer service smile fell. I remembered having seen her after Patrick and I left the theater, and she was standing on the corner and scowling at me. *Did she follow us? And how did she know I worked here?*

I swallowed a lump in my throat. This woman was potentially dangerous. I didn't know yet if she was the kind to follow through with threats or just make them. I needed to be on my guard.

But I thought about what little Patrick had said about her, that she was different than he thought she was. Maybe she had hidden this side from him and hated him for finally discovering it and leaving him for it. There was no way sweet and easygoing Patrick could date someone like her, right?

"Why should I stay away from Patrick?" I asked her. So far, I was keeping my cool.

She scoffed. "Isn't it obvious that he and I belong together?"

I looked her up and down. She wore a bright blue leather trench coat with fur around the neck and sleeves, pointed high-heeled boots, and her ears were adorned with dangling diamond earrings. I had a feeling that she thought she could get whatever she wanted just by telling someone rudely that she wanted it. She probably hadn't been told no even once in her life.

I was looking at a spoiled rich girl who just wanted attention. And that type of character always peeved me. When reading, I wondered why it was hard for some people to stand up to them, but now was my opportunity to try.

"No," I said plainly. "It's not obvious at all."

Emily, that was her name. I had forgotten for a moment. Emily deepened her scowl, a challenging smile spreading slowly across her face. "Well then, since you seem to be so ignorant, I'll spell it out for you. Patrick is, and always has been, my boyfriend."

I stared at her. She was delusional. I almost felt sorry for her.

"Just stop messing with my boyfriend," she said with a low growl.

I crossed my arms and just looked at her. "The way I see it," I said, "you two have been broken up for over a year. Patrick is trying to be happy and find someone better, but you're just embarrassing him and stressing him out with your obsessive behavior."

Every trace of Emily's smile dropped and her mouth fell agape. "How dare you!" she spat back. "You're the one who's embarrassing him, what with that little cutesy graduation dinner. What an embarrassing scene having the whole restaurant sing for you, making all of those strangers celebrate your graduation. That's so absurd."

I hadn't witnessed such a spectacle of the green-eyed monster before. She was jealous. She probably knew that Patrick was a good guy and that she was crazy for letting him go. She probably wished that all of those people in the restaurant were celebrating her. Again, I almost felt sorry for her.

"Listen," I said firmly. "You can think what you want. But you are not going to cheapen that day for me. I had no say in that celebration at the restaurant. Patrick wanted to surprise me when he found out that I was officially graduating. It was a really sweet thing for him to do, and it was really nice that everyone—of their own free will—to decide to join in and sing. It was a little embarrassing for me because I didn't expect the attention, but it also meant a lot to me. It was special, and you can't make it less than that with your drama and your little threats."

Emily stared at me wide-eyed. She seemed to be in disbelief. Maybe nobody had ever spoken to her like that before. "You—"

"Get it through your head," I said, interrupting her. "You're not his girlfriend anymore."

She scoffed, trying to recover from her bout of silence. "What you say doesn't matter. What he says doesn't matter. Because *I'm* not letting him go."

"This isn't love," I told her. "He deserves better."

"Oh, and you think you're better than me?" she shot back loudly.

I glanced around the bookstore, remembering we were still in my place of work. I didn't want to cause a big scene, but someone had caught our little exchange and one of the team leaders was heading over. Even though I wasn't in the wrong, I was worried how Emily might try to twist it to make me look like a bad guy. I just wanted her to leave.

"All I can say is he deserves better than you," I said. "Now you need to leave."

"Well, I'll have you know that I have power! Do you know who my dad is? All I have to do is say the word and my father can ruin that little electric business of his if he doesn't come back to me," she said. She really thought that was an option, threatening him with destroying the business he'd created.

I thought about my parents and how hard they had worked to get the bakery up and running all on their own. I imagined that for Patrick, building his business had been the same.

"That's ridiculous," I told her. "There's a reason he left. If you want him to love you, this is not how to go about it."

"Is everything okay here?" the team leader asked as she approached.

Emily flicked her wicked eyes at innocent Samantha and huffed before storming away.

"Are you okay?" Samantha asked me. "What happened?"

I could tell she was a bit worried about receiving complaints and having to deal with that, and I hoped it wouldn't go that far. But I didn't know Emily. I also didn't trust her, and I knew I wouldn't put anything past her.

"It's just a personal vendetta," I said. "I don't think you have anything to worry about."

Samantha looked at me with pity, or maybe it was just concern and I was pitying myself. "Are you sure you're okay, though? She seemed very rude."

I gave a short half-hearted laugh. "Is it okay if I take my break now?"

Samantha nodded and took over the register for me. I wasn't sure how far Emily would go on her little rampage, but I thought it would be best for Patrick to know that she was out there causing trouble and that she had followed us on our—well, I still didn't know if it was a date or not.

I made my way to the break room to grab my coat and gloves before stepping outside into the brisk winter air. It hadn't snowed for a little while, and the snow on the ground was starting to get mixed up with mud and debris. It wasn't so pretty.

I took out my phone and pulled up Patrick's contact.

"Holly!" he answered cheerfully.

CHAPTER 12

Patrick

I WAS EXCITED to receive another call from Holly. She'd just asked about the gingerbread house thing, so I wondered what else she wanted to do with me. I found myself hoping that she'd ask me on another date. I knew I could ask her too, but guys were allowed to get excited for the woman to take charge once in a while.

"Holly!" I answered, probably too cheerfully.

"Hey," she said. Her voice was strained, without its usual lightness.

My heart sank. Was she canceling? "What's up?" I asked. I knew jumping to conclusions was never the route to go.

"Have you seen your ex lately?" she asked.

It was like someone dropped a brick into my stomach. "Emily? She paid me a visit yesterday." I gulped, not knowing whether I wanted to know the answer to my next question or not. "Why's that?"

Holly was quiet for a moment, and that stirred up some discomfort in my chest.

"Holly?" I asked, hoping to prompt her along.

"She paid me a visit, too," she said.

I was shocked. "What? When?"

Holly chuckled without emotion. "Just now, at the bookstore."

"While you were working?" I asked, the discomfort twisting into anger. Coming after me with her petty begging was one thing, but to go after Holly–I couldn't have that.

"Yeah," Holly said.

I couldn't tell if she sounded sad or disappointed. I wished I could see her face so I'd have a better idea about how she was feeling. "Are you okay? What'd she say? What'd she do?"

Holly explained that Emily had come in and told her to stay away from me, that I was and always had been her boyfriend.

"I'm so sorry," I said.

I had come to know how Emily could be. She used to be sweet and demure and kind, but all of that was a lie, a mask. I knew how vicious she could be, how disrespectful and harsh she could be. My heart wrenched. Holly was the last person who deserved to be subject to that kind of behavior.

Holly sighed. "It's not your fault. She's just… obsessed."

I knew that, especially over the last few weeks. But hearing someone else say it made the news hit a little harder. Maybe I was still trying to come to terms with the kind of person Emily had turned out to be. I had been so sure she was nice in the beginning. It was hard to be so wrong about someone.

"I'll talk to her," I said. I felt exhausted just saying the words.

"Wait," Holly said. She hesitated again. "There's something else she said."

I gritted my teeth.

"She said that she had power, that she could talk to her dad and ruin your business. Would she really do something like that?"

I was getting so mad, and this just sent me over the edge. Not only was Emily following me around, but now she was targeting a woman I was interested in, spreading lies around town, and threatening my job. Not only that, but she was trying to use her own family to do it when I knew that her parents were not the kind of people who would do something like that.

"Don't pay her any mind," I told Holly. "That's probably an empty threat. She thinks since her dad is one of the businessmen in town that she can use him to get anything she wants, but despite being a rich businessman, I've never known him or his wife to treat anyone unfairly. That's one of the reasons why I didn't realize...." I trailed off. Emily's parents were good people, stand-up citizens, down to earth. So, it was difficult for me to believe that Emily had turned out to be so... corrupt.

"Are you sure?" Holly asked. "I don't want her to take anything else away from you."

My heart sprung awake again. *Holly was worried about me? She cared about me in that kind of way?* I cleared my throat and tried to wrangle my thoughts.

"Yeah. I'll be fine," I said. "You're free to worry about me, though, if you feel inclined."

I hoped Holly was smiling on the other end of the line. "You just deserve to be happy," she said. "I want you to be happy."

What was this woman saying all of a sudden? My heart triple-thumped in my chest and heat rose up through my neck. *Did she know what she was doing to me?*

"Oh! I forgot something else important," she said suddenly.

My heart stopped again. Maybe Holly was more dangerous to my heart than Emily was....

"I saw her that night. The night we were... uh... together, you know, at the movies," Holly explained.

That was cute. *Was she afraid to call it a date?* I thought about that night and how I felt now. We should just call it what it was. "You mean our date?"

Holly grew quiet again. She cleared her throat lightly before she spoke again, and her voice sounded light and free again. "Yeah. Our date...."

"I figured as much. When she came to me, she said something about 'the scene in the restaurant.'"

"I hope you didn't let her make you think that that was stupid or embarrassing," Holly said. "Because it wasn't. I really enjoyed that. I enjoyed every part of that night."

My chest was thumping away again. *Did I forget how to swallow?*

"I'm glad you had a good time," I managed to say. "I'm glad I could make you smile."

Holly let out a cute, short giggle. "Well, I loved it. I'm sorry I didn't thank you until now."

"We can talk about a proper thank you when I see you tomorrow," I said. "I'll be judging your gingerbread making skills."

Holly guffawed. "Yeah? Well, I'll have you know that if we compete, you don't stand a chance. I've been making gingerbread houses every year since I was four."

I grinned. Holly was so fun, and she cared about me. She loved Christmas just as much as I did, and she seemed like a genuinely good person. Then again, I had been wrong about a woman before.

"Challenge accepted," I told her. I noted the flirty tone of my voice and told myself to get it together.

Holly sighed. "Well, then, I look forward to seeing you."

I could hear the smile in her voice. I wondered if she was smiling big enough to see that little dimple on her cheek. I held my phone tightly. It was getting harder to get a grip on my feelings. "Same," I said.

"Good news?" Andrew asked with a smug grin when I hung up after saying goodbye.

We had met for lunch at a burger joint and he had a French fry dangling from his mouth. I tossed one of my tater tots at him. "Not exactly."

He fumbled around for the tater tot and popped it in his mouth. "Coulda fooled me."

I thought about the mystery woman again. She was still there in the back of my mind. And the intense kiss we'd shared under the mistletoe still sprung up in my mind almost daily. I wondered again if I should be spending so much time with Holly.

At least, maybe I should try to figure out the mystery woman thing before letting Holly tug at my heart strings some more. I stood up from the table suddenly. Tomorrow was the gingerbread house volunteer day. I needed to figure it out before then.

"What are you doing?" Andrew asked.

"I need to go somewhere," I told him.

I tossed some money from my wallet onto the table and left Andrew to settle the bill. I crawled into my cold truck and drove to Noel right away. I'd questioned myself the first time, but maybe I just wasn't asking the right questions.

I was sure I had seen the van correctly, so I was going to go back to Kris Kringle's Cookies and find out just who was in that van that night. She had to be connected to that place somehow.

The drive felt longer than usual, but I arrived at Noel in record time. I thought it might be perfect timing to catch the owner, but despite being there at two in the afternoon when there should have been a break in business, the bakery was still quite busy.

This time, I didn't see the younger man at the cash register. Instead, it was an older woman, possibly nearing her sixties. She looked familiar.

I waited in line behind a customer who had ordered twelve dozen cross cookies for their church. It took a while for the lady to settle the bill, and then the woman went to the back to fetch the order. I wondered how she was going to bring out a dozen boxes herself, but an older man followed behind her. When I saw their two faces together, I placed them as the couple who had been manning the cookie table at the toy drive. Then I remembered that I had waved to them the first time I was here. But I had never spoken to them.

The older lady apologized when she made it back around the counter. "So sorry it took me so long to get to you, young man. My extra hands are out today on account of his wife having a baby!"

I smiled. "Oh, that's okay."

"What can I do for you? Did you have an order?" she asked.

I shook my head. "No. Sorry, but I just wanted to ask a few questions. Can I speak with the owner of the place?"

The lady hooked her thumbs in the pockets of her apron and gleamed up at me. "You're talking to her!"

"Oh!" I said, feeling a bit sorry. "I didn't realize."

She shrugged. "Eh, I'm about to retire anyway. Well, maybe in a couple years—don't tell my husband."

I laughed. She had a familiar kind of humor. Her demeanor and her gestures reminded me of someone....

The door dinged behind me and the lady welcomed the customers in. She asked them to wait a moment, but I didn't want to interrupt their business for these questions. "Go ahead and help them out. I'll just wait until you have a moment."

"Why, that's so kind. Thanks, young man," she said.

As I waited for a few minutes while she did her job, I looked around at the place. It was decked out for Christmas. I had a feeling that, given the name of this place, it never lost its Christmas charm. We did live in the most Christmassy place in the world it seemed. But I appreciated the homey decor–the pictures on the wall of the bakery the day it opened, a little tawny girl with pigtails standing on a chair helping to mix cookies. Maybe she had a daughter.

I watched the woman work. She was kind and seemed to be a dedicated worker, but I could see the tiredness in her eyes. It was hidden in the wrinkles of her smile lines. She finished up with her customer and came around the counter to chat with me.

"Sorry for the interruption. What kind of questions did you have?" she asked.

I glanced around the place. "How'd you come to open your own bakery?" I found myself asking.

She smiled gently, not swayed in the slightest by my random question. "My grandmother taught me how to bake," she explained. "It was the most fun I ever had. I developed quite a sweet tooth because of her. I wanted to make every cookie under the sun so I could share them with my friends. I suppose I never let go of that dream even as I got older. Then I met my husband, and he helped me officially get started. We've been full throttle ever since then."

It was a simple story, but it was sweet, relatable.

"Why the Christmas theme?" I asked.

She chuckled a little. "Oh, son, that's just my family! All of us have always loved Christmas, every aspect of it. I even met my husband at the Santa Claus Ball!"

That got my attention. And it was the perfect timing to ask her—

The front door dinged again. In rushed a customer with a panicked expression, and another stressed lady ran in behind her carrying a smashed cake on a platter. "Please help us! This is my sister's wedding cake. I just picked it up earlier, but I slipped on the ice and dropped it before I got it home to put in the fridge."

The woman was full-on crying. I couldn't imagine how she must feel. I knew women were usually picky about wedding stuff, at least all of the women I'd known. And to ruin someone else's wedding cake, especially your sister's–yikes.

"I'm so, so sorry," she said to me. "Do you mind waiting? Or… maybe another time would be better for your questions."

I didn't want to intrude. I'd already distracted her enough from her work. I started to leave but the woman caught my arm.

"Wait! Here! Take this." She reached over the counter and grabbed a plastic-wrapped cookie. There was a business card tied to it with a silver ribbon. "It's on the house."

I was two for two. The last time I was there, a man had given me a free cookie. And now this–I liked this place. I thought I might like to go back even if I didn't meet my mystery woman there.

On the way back to Mistletoe Mountain, I thought about Holly. It was beginning to seem like this mystery woman and I were only connected through a single kiss. It was beautiful and meaningful, but maybe that was all that it was. Maybe I had been trying too hard to make something out of it when I should have started dedicating my time elsewhere.

I decided from then on, I was just going to enjoy my time with Holly. I wasn't going to put pressure on either side.

CHAPTER 13

Holly

SOMETHING in my gut was telling me to go for it with Patrick. I really enjoyed his company, I felt like I could talk to him forever, and he most definitely wasn't bad to look at. Sure, he had a little baggage as did anyone, and Emily was a pretty big piece of baggage, but all in all, I didn't find a single reason why he couldn't potentially be better than my velvet-suited mystery man. At least, it wasn't unreasonable to continue hanging out with him. Right?

I was honestly surprised and proud that I had asked him to join me at the gingerbread house building event. But after talking to him some more at the toy drive and finding out that he loved Christmas almost as much as me, I thought it would be better to ask him than to drag along Abigail, who would say yes but drag her feet, or to even attempt to get Gretchen to pull herself away from her boyfriend long enough. Patrick and I were alike in that aspect, and that excited me.

And... after the date, of course, especially after he'd termed it a date during our phone call, I felt like we might have more in common after all. Whether or not I ever found my velvet-suited Santa, it couldn't be a bad thing to want to spend more time with Patrick.

We'd decided to drive to the event separately, given our differing work schedules and all, but I spotted him right away when he walked in. He was wearing a red plaid button up shirt and, as usual, well-fitting jeans. It seemed like he might have trimmed his hair a bit, but it was still a little shaggy. With it trimmed back a little off of his forehead, his beautiful blue eyes were more visible, more prominent. I found myself just staring into them as he approached me.

"Everything okay?" he asked.

I shook my head, trying to reel my mind back in. "Just happy to see you," I said.

I thought I caught some redness tinge the tips of his ears. "Is that right? You missed my face?"

I chuckled. "Not at all. I just needed a nice, tall guy like you to help me out."

His ego deflated slightly, but he didn't lose his smile or sense of humor. "You know I've got the muscles to go with it."

I didn't doubt that, but I just shrugged nonchalantly to tease him. "You don't really need muscle to lift tinsel."

He sniffed. "Well, then…."

One of the other volunteers came by and started delegating tasks. The three of us worked together for a while putting up the decorations in the community center before more people arrived to help. As I was adding the finishing touches to the tables and triple-checking the supplies, our first kid arrived. He was a timid little boy of about nine, clinging to his mom's hand.

Patrick was fixing up the faux-snow-covered garland around the doorway when the kid came through. The boy stopped in the doorway and looked around hesitantly. His mom crouched down and spoke to him sweetly, probably helping to nurse his nerves.

Then I witnessed something quite cute. Patrick must have also noticed the boy's anxiety. He scraped off a little bit of the faux snow into his hand and sprinkled it in the air so that it fell like real snow.

The little boy's eyes brightened when he saw the little bits of white trickling down from above, falling into his hair and on the floor. His mother looked up and the little boy's gaze followed. Patrick was already climbing down the ladder. He wore a jolly smile and spoke with calm excitement. I didn't catch everything he said, but whatever it was helped the kid to let go of his mom's hand and take Patrick's instead.

My heart warmed at the sight. It seemed like Patrick really understood the depth of the Christmas spirit. I really appreciated that, especially since it seemed so hard to find nowadays. My heart tugged in my chest. Patrick was amazing and I really did like him, so why was that kiss under the mistletoe still popping up in my head?

Suddenly, Abigail appeared next to me. She literally spooked me, and I dropped one of the decorative balls. Thankfully, it was plastic, so it didn't break. But I did catch everyone's gaze when the thing bounced like a ping pong ball across the floor. The little boy stopped it with the toe of his boot before picking it up. Patrick whispered something to him, and he shook his head. Then they were heading over.

"What the heck are you doing here?" I asked Abigail. "I thought you weren't going to come."

She smiled smugly. "I wanted to check things out, you know?"

I eyed her suspiciously as Patrick and the boy neared us. "Don't be weird," I told her.

Her grin spread evilly.

The two stopped in front of us and Patrick gestured to us. "Brody here wanted to give this back to you and to tell you something, Holly."

I bent down slightly to retrieve the plastic ball from the boy's hand. He just had his arm sticking out at me while his eyes were nervously darting around the floor, avoiding my gaze. "Hello, Brody," I said. "Thanks for being so kind and bringing this back to me."

He made the slightest nod with his head.

I thought that was all, but Patrick didn't turn to leave. Instead, he whispered in the boy's ear and gave him a soft pat on the back. I met eyes with Patrick and he just smiled and nodded once. I took it as a sign to be patient.

Maybe Brody just needed a little more conversation to warm up before he would speak. "Are you excited to make—"

"You're really pretty!" Brody said suddenly. Then he tore away from Patrick and ran back toward his mother, who was signing him in near the door and chatting with the lead organizer.

Abigail nudged me in the arm while Patrick just grinned at me.

"What was that all about?" I said to Patrick. "Did you make him say that?"

Patrick just shrugged. "Hey, we might have shared the same thought, but he's the one who wanted to tell you."

My cheeks flushed immediately. *Did Patrick just second-handedly tell me I was pretty?* I placed the plastic ball on the table and quickly tried to busy myself at the next table. "Don't mess around," I told him. "The boy seems shy enough."

Patrick chuckled and left it alone. He went back to the doorway to put the ladder away.

"Patrick. The guy from the volunteer day at the park?" Abigail asked.

I nodded.

"Patrick. The guy you went on a potential date with to celebrate your graduation?"

I nodded again.

"Patrick. The guy you're in love with?"

I spun around, aghast. "I am not!"

Abigail snickered. "I was just checking."

I rolled my eyes and bumped her with my hip as I walked by her. She matched my step and followed me to the tables on the far side of the room.

"Hey, but if we can't find your mystery guy, I think Patrick is a good match, too. He seems into you," she said.

I tried to ignore the heat in my face. I flicked my gaze at her, wondering how much longer she was going to tease me about him.

"It's too bad I didn't catch any leads yet. I've been asking all the other guys if they kissed a green-pinned Mrs. Claus at the Santa Claus Ball."

I froze. "You've been doing what now?"

Abigail answered nonchalantly. "I've been asking them if they kissed a girl wearing a green pin. That's you in case you forgot."

I felt my jaw dropping slowly in disbelief. So much for ignoring that heat in my face….

"That is so embarrassing!" I said. "Why would you—"

"Relax, girl. Nobody knows that it's you. They probably think it's me if anything," she said. "And that could actually be hurting your chances since I'm not as cute and demure as you."

It was true. Abigail was more edgy. She was the friend who didn't give two rats' tails what anyone had to say or think.

"Still!" I said. "What if Patrick hears that you've been asking around? He might think…."

"Think what? That you kissed someone else?"

I gritted my teeth.

"Or, hey!" she nearly shouted. "What if I go ask him?"

"Don't you dare!" I said, grabbing the open button side of her sweater. I glared at her, but I didn't think I'd scared her at all.

"Hey!" What if it's him?" she said, wiggling her eyebrows.

I scoffed. "Don't you think I would have figured it out by now if it was?"

"Yeah, maybe," she said.

A strained silence hung between us until I let go of her sweater and started to relax. It would be nice if she found him, I thought. Maybe it wasn't such a bad thing that she was asking around for me. The sooner I found him, the sooner I could feel comfortable deciding what to do with my growing feelings for Patrick.

I glanced at Patrick across the room. He was now surrounded by a group of six-year-old girls. They were pulling on his shirt hem and grabbing onto his legs.

"You really didn't get any leads?" I muttered.

Abigail answered surprisingly sincerely. "No. Sorry, girl. I'm really trying."

"I know," I told her. I laid my head on her shoulder for a split second, remembering that she wasn't generally the kind to show affection physically.

"At any rate," I said, handing her a few packages of gumdrops and candy canes. "Maybe cool it with the questions for now. At least don't do it while I'm around. It's way too embarrassing, even if they don't know you're asking for me."

Abigail laughed. "Okay, Holly. I'll ask behind your back then."

As the gingerbread event kicked off, I thought a little bit about what might change if I ever found my velvet-suited mystery man. I let my gaze travel to Patrick, who caught my eyes and smiled. *Would I have to stop seeing him? Or would I have to abandon the man who had stirred up such a magical sensation in me in only a few minutes?*

I wondered if it would take a lot of work to keep seeing Patrick, especially if things were to become more romantic. I had a feeling Emily would not take kindly to it. But then again, as I watched him play with the kids and give his whole heart and imagination to them, I couldn't help but feel that he might be worth that little bit of trouble.

If only I knew more about the mystery man....

As I thought about it, I came to a semi-conclusion. If my Santa Claus match and I were meant to be together, then we'd find each other somehow. If that magic between us was real, then it was guaranteed. And if it wasn't, then... maybe reality wouldn't be so bad.

"Hey, Holly," Patrick said, coming up to me later as we were finishing up.

I was happy to have him by my side for that moment, even if we were just packing things away in boxes together. "Hey, Patrick. Did you have a good time?"

He nodded. "Of course. Getting to let go and be a kid again was so fun."

I grinned at him. He had an innocent love for Christmas and cheer that I admired. "Even though you cheated and made a car instead of a house?"

He gasped dramatically. "Cheated? Why I would never!"

"You didn't follow the rules," I insisted. "You could have helped that kid win the competition, but you didn't follow the rules."

He clicked his tongue. "Psh. As the official Professional at Fun and Toys, I don't think I have to follow the rules. That's what takes the fun out of things, you see."

"Well, still. That poor boy and his broken heart. I bet he really would have liked to win," I said.

The play guilting wasn't working. "Hah! His heart wasn't broken! He was amazed! I think this newfound skill will get him a lot of ladies in art class in a couple of years."

I nearly cracked up. "Oh, is that the goal here?"

"That depends. You seemed pretty impressed. Did it work on you?" he asked slyly.

I turned around so he couldn't see my smile. "I like a guy who has fun inside the rules."

Patrick sighed heavily and drooped his head. "I thought you might have admired the creativity."

I stared at him blankly and just shook my head, laughing.

CHAPTER 14

Patrick

I HAD a great time talking to Holly. She made me feel light and carefree. And our shared love of Christmas just made our time together so easy and natural. Plus, I was really starting to see her beauty. Maybe thoughts of the mystery woman had me distracted, because Holly really was quite beautiful. I loved the way her hair fell over her shoulders, the way her green eyes brightened. I loved the faint appearance of freckles splattered over her nose and the shape of her lips. Then there was that sneaky little dimple. I loved catching sight of it when she let go of a big smile.

After we'd cleaned up the community center from the gingerbread building event, I found myself wanting to hang out with her a little while longer. So I decided to throw caution to the wind and just do it.

"What are you doing tonight?" I asked her.

She seemed a little shocked by my question. "Oh, I was just going to go home," she said.

I didn't think that was a passive remark about actually wanting to go home. So I went out on a limb and asked a follow up question. "How do you feel about walks in the cold?"

Holly pinched her eyebrows together slightly, but a little crook of a smile flicked at the corner of her mouth. "That depends how far it is," she said hesitantly.

"Until you want to stop," he said. "We'll go until you say the word."

She was quiet, like she was really mulling something over in her head. I obviously didn't want to pressure her, but I did want to spend more time with her.

"There will be lots of Christmas lights," I said with a lilting voice.

She gave a light chuckle. "How can I say no to that?"

I grabbed Holly's emerald green coat and helped her shoulder it on. I knew she could do it herself, but I just wanted to do it. I watched her take her gloves out of her pocket and slide her slender hands into them. I shrugged on my coat too, but I regretted not having a scarf or something.

"Here," Holly said, unraveling her scarf from the coat rack. "You look like you need an extra layer."

"Oh, you don't have to worry about me," I said.

Holly frowned, then lifted up on her tippy toes and raised her arms over my head. The front of her coat bumped me as she wound the scarf around my head a couple of times. It was plush and colored gray and it smelled like her. This was the first time I was getting such a clear whiff of her scent. It was like cranberries and pine needles and cinnamon. She smelled like Christmas.

I couldn't help but grin.

"What?" she asked. "Are you ashamed to wear a ladies scarf? I think it looks good on you."

I shook my head. "No. It's not that." But I chose not to explain the real reason I was smiling. It was like this woman was the embodiment of Christmas itself.

"Well, are you ready then?" she asked.

I nodded. Instinctively I reached out for her hand, but she had already taken off. It was probably for the best. We'd only been out together a couple of times, after all.

Then again... I'd kissed my mystery Mrs. Claus after talking to her for just a few minutes. I had felt so sure then that that woman was something special. The moment I caught sight of her in the crowd, it was like there was a glow around her.

Holly had a similar glow. It must have been her general cheery demeanor and her excitement for the holidays.

I followed Holly out of the door and caught up to her on the snowy sidewalk.

"I wish it'd snow again and make the world all white and clean," Holly said.

I stuck my hands in my pockets before I accidentally made any more surprise moves. "Right? I love how clear and pure the world looks right after a good snow. Driving past a big open field and not seeing a speck of imperfection–it's just so beautiful."

Holly smiled up at me. "And the way the bare trees brighten back up and sparkle with icicles and little puffs of snow."

"Is winter your favorite season?" I asked her.

She nodded. "It has to be. It's the season of my favorite holiday."

"Is Christmas your favorite holiday then?"

She looked ornery. "No. It's my birthday."

"What? Your birthday? Is it coming up then?" I asked. I hoped it was. That would give me another excuse to see her later on.

She lost her ornery grin and sighed instead. "Actually it's passed. It's technically not even in the winter. It's in November, but I like to pretend it's in the same season. It's about a month off."

"So you just had your birthday then?"

She nodded.

I pressed my hands a bit deeper into my pockets. "I'll have to get you a belated gift!"

She scoffed. "Please, between the graduation stuff and... well... this, I guess, you've done plenty."

"Next year then," I muttered.

Holly's gaze flicked up to me again shortly before returning to the houses around us. We both let the conversation come to a gentle pause as we walked side by side and admired the houses along main street and the decorations in the yards.

Maybe it was because of the name and location of Mistletoe Mountain, but it seemed like the majority of the town held Christmas in the same regard. Nearly every home was lined with colorful strings of lights. That was the bare minimum effort most people seemed to put in. Many houses were totally decked out with inflatables and yard ornaments, or others had decorated a tree in their yard like a giant Christmas tree, kind of how we'd done with the ones in the park. Lots of houses also had snowmen or mini igloos sporting their yards. And in every window, I could see the family's Christmas tree lit up and shining.

"What makes you love Christmas so much?" Holly asked suddenly. Her voice was soft and curious, like she was asking me something secretive.

I cleared my throat lightly before answering. "Well, it reminds me of my family."

It was a sensitive topic, but I didn't mind sharing with her.

"Do you have a big family?" she asked.

I shook my head. "It's just my aunt and me."

"Oh," Holly said sadly. "Can I ask…. Where are your parents?"

I slowed a bit. I didn't mind sharing, but it was sudden. Holly slowed, too, and looked up at me from under her brown lashes.

"A few years ago, my parents both died in an accident. Well, my mother died on impact, and my dad only lasted a couple of days in critical condition after that. But I think he knew she was gone and he didn't want to be here without her," I told her. I felt my throat begin to tighten up, which was unexpected. Of course, I was still upset that my parents were dead, but I hadn't cried about it in a while.

Holly gasped lightly and looped her arm through mine. "That must be so hard. I can't imagine."

Most people said, "that must *have been* so hard," putting the tragedy in the past. But Holly didn't. And she was right. It *was* hard, currently, especially during the holidays.

"Yeah," I admitted. "It is. But I know they'd be upset if I didn't carry on loving Christmas like I did when I was a kid, like when we were all together."

"Is it hard? To keep loving Christmas without them?" she asked. "If it weren't for them, would you still love Christmas like you did when you were a kid?"

I'd never thought about it like that before. "I'm not sure," I said honestly. "But I think so. You see, I was eighteen when they passed. Actually, I'd just graduated high school. And I think I was the only boy in school who admittedly claimed to be excited about Christmas. It wasn't just about the gifts or the food or the time away from school like most kids felt. Christmas just felt so… whole."

I glanced down at Holly. She was looking straight ahead now. I spied a single tear streaking down her cheek, but I didn't want to call attention to it.

"Anyway," I continued, "my grandparents passed from heart attacks long ago, and now that my parents are gone too, my aunt and I have a small Christmas together, but I've started filling it up with more events and more volunteering."

I hoped to start filling it up with a family of my own. I thought I might have had that with Emily, but that clearly turned out not to be the case. So for now, it was just me and my aunt, and maybe this year I'd have Mrs. Henson, too. And, if luck would have it, I might spend a little time with my friends or… even with Holly.

She let out a long breath. "You're so strong," she said. "If my parents were gone, I'd probably be the opposite. I'd probably hate Christmas because of all of the pain of missing them."

I gave Holly's arm a light squeeze with mine. I wanted to comfort her. "I do miss them. And it does hurt," I said. "But I can't let one terrible thing overshadow all of the great memories we made. I don't want it to stop me from making great new memories."

I brought us to a stop in front of the little park at the city's center. There was a small frozen-over pond that a few people were walking laps around. It was like a picture from Norman Rockwell.

"Look," I said, gesturing with my arm. "The world is still beautiful. Rather than feeling sorry all of the time, I try to give thanks. I thank

God for the time I had with my parents and my grandparents. I give thanks for the way they raised me. I can't say that I don't feel sad about it. It's natural to. But now I get to enjoy life for all of us."

"What's your favorite memory?" Holly asked quietly. She leaned slightly against my arm.

I smiled as I recalled the story. It was one of my favorites because it happened nearly every year. "There was this one time," I began as I thought back. "My grandparents were still alive. I only ever had the one set, as my mom was a bit estranged from her family. But my dad had this bright idea to go sledding in my grandparents' field like he used to when he was a kid. There was this big hill that was perfect for it, just steep enough to send you flying halfway across the field. I was probably eight at the time, and I thought it sounded like so much fun, so of course I was advocating for it. My mom and grandma stood on the porch to keep an eye on us in case someone did something reckless.

"Well, my dad was the ornery type," I continued. "Maybe he was making up for something, but he just acted like a big kid sometimes. So my grandpa gets out a couple of old sleds, one for me and one for my dad. He gives me the red one because it was my favorite color, and he took the yellow one. I was a bit nervous because as a kid that hill looked a little scary at first, so I watched my dad slide down the hill. He took a running start and everything. But he looked so cool, like a superhero. The snow was slinging off the back of the sled as he zoomed down. I just couldn't wait to try it too.

"All my nerves turned to adrenaline, and I took off after my dad. My grandpa tried to catch me when he saw me start to run, but he slipped and I got away. I took the biggest, bravest leap of my life off the side of that hill and I *crashed* into the snow. I immediately lost control but gained speed, and the next thing I knew, I got flung off the sled and got sent tumbling down the side. My dad had apparently come to a stop and witnessed me tumbling down the hill, so he ran up to stop me. My mom was also there in a flash, without a sweater and with her house slippers full of snow.

"I broke my arm that day. And my mom fretted over me. She

scolded my dad for the rest of his life about that. But that next winter, my dad showed me the proper way and my mom found us having races down the hill. We both got scolded, but eventually, my dad convinced my mom to give it a try, and soon enough, we were all sledding down that hill together with grandma at the bottom declaring the winner. It was something of a tradition until my grandparents died and we had to sell the farm."

I sighed. I hadn't shared that story for a long time. It still made my heart happy to remember it. I really had a lot of great memories with my family. It was tough that they were no longer around to continue making memories with me, but I was grateful nonetheless.

After a moment of silence, I heard Holly sniffle. I twisted to face her. We stood toe to toe. Holly's nose was pink and her eyes were welled up with tears.

I laughed gently. And took my hands out of my pocket, placing one hand carefully on the side of her neck, my thumb brushing her jawline. I dabbed at her tear with the hook of my index finger. "So, you're a softie, huh?"

She gave a short sad laugh and tried to look away. But I caught her chin and urged her to look back at me. She was reluctant at first. Then she locked on to my eyes.

"Thank you for listening," I told her.

She batted her eyes, maybe fighting more tears away. I didn't want her to cry, but it touched me that my family's story moved her.

I brushed her cheek with my thumb. "I really like that you have a big heart," I told her.

I studied her lips, wondering if this was the right time. *Was it too soon?*

Then Holly inched forward and parted her lips slightly. That was a signal, right? She placed her hands on my jacket pockets and I knew it. I wanted to kiss her, and I thought she wanted to kiss me too.

Suddenly, a child cried out, "Mommy! It's snowing! It's snowing!"

Holly and I jerked back simultaneously. She shoved her hands quickly into her pockets and stepped back. I put my hands back in my pockets, too, and tried to will my heart back into a normal rhythm.

"It really is snowing," Holly said.

I looked up. Sure enough, big, thick flurries were falling from the grayish sky. It looked like we were both going to get that clean slate of snow that we wanted.

"Hey," I said, bumping her with my elbow. "You wanna join in?"

She looked in the direction I gestured. A couple of kids were building a snowman while some teenagers began to throw balls of snow at each other.

Holly grinned with playful malice. "I have killer aim," she said.

Then she took off in their direction.

Before I went after her, I thought about how nice it would have been to kiss her. Maybe it would have erased the mystery woman's lingering kiss from my memory. Maybe we could have started something great....

Then again, a moment like this was pretty great, too.

CHAPTER 15

Holly

I WAS PRACTICALLY FLOATING like a snowflake on the wind in the morning, still high off of my winter night walk with Patrick. I was so touched that he felt comfortable enough to open up to me about his family. He had had a tough time losing all of these people who were so important to him. It was so gut-wrenchingly beautiful that he'd maintained such a bright outlook on life and such a cheery disposition in spite of these major losses.

I couldn't imagine what it would be like. I still had both of my parents and all my grandparents. It just didn't seem fair. But I was amazed by Patrick. I looked up to him in that regard. He was truly a great guy.

Then there was that moment we almost kissed. At least, it really seemed like that was what was about to happen, before the kids in the park started whooping and hollering, anyway.

As I worked through the morning, I thought about that night. I wondered what made him want to be so vulnerable with me. I wondered how we could have connected so quickly. *Was it the same kind of magic that happened between me and the velvet-suited mystery man?*

Though Patrick and I had been getting to know each other more slowly, it was still quick. We'd only known each other a couple of weeks. Or maybe....

"Holly."

My thoughts were cut off by my manager calling out to me. I switched my attention to her. "Yes?"

"I need you to move to gift wrapping duty, okay? Caroline will be covering the register," she explained.

Honestly, I was excited to move to gift wrapping. Stocking or working the register was okay, but gift wrapping was where all the fun was. It was the best place in the house to hone in on the Christmas spirit and share it. I loved wrapping presents, and I had the skill for making the perfect folds and crisp straight lines. Plus I got to add little ribbons and strings and decorations to make it fancier, to give it more character.

Altogether, the bookstore's atmosphere was on point with peak Christmastime. It was officially only two weeks until Christmas. Outside and around town, people were hustling and bustling to get gifts and make plans with family, but they were also just enjoying the snow and the community activities.

Between customer gifts, I got to create little gift baskets that could be purchased. I put together books and games and coffee mugs and cute miscellaneous items. I had a lot of fun doing it.

I had hit a busy streak for a while. Then I thought it was going to calm down, but right before lunchtime, I got swamped. There was a line of about six customers who were waiting for me to wrap their gifts. Then I got another visitor.

"Hey," a man's voice sounded from beside me.

I swiveled around quickly. "Patrick? What are you doing here?" I asked. I was totally surprised to see him so suddenly—and unexpectedly. I hadn't seen him since that night, the night we'd almost kissed. His sudden appearance brought heat to my cheeks.

"Just wanted to drop by," he began, then he slowly added, "to see you."

I gulped. So I hadn't imagined that night. If those kids hadn't yelped with excitement, we would have....

"So what are you doing over here?" he asked.

I was glad he asked me a direct question. I wasn't sure how to respond to his previous statement. I cleared my throat. "Uh, well, I'm just making gift baskets. As you can see, I've got a few people waiting, so it might not be a good time...."

"Is it against the rules to help out?" he asked, starting to shuffle around the counter.

How peculiar, I thought. *He just wanted to help out? What brought him here in the first place?*

"I thought you didn't care about the rules?" I teased. Then I slid my finished present to my customer, who took it with a smile.

Patrick shrugged. "That was for a competition. There's no winning this time. Just... helping out."

I narrowed my eyes. "You're not working?"

Patrick shook his head. Then he greeted the next customer.

"How do I know your wrapping skills are up to par?" I muttered, leaning toward him. "I have high standards, and a legacy to protect."

Patrick just winked at me. "Trust me, love."

I was too stunned, and my heart was too fluttery for me to respond. I just blinked and tried my best to look normal. My mom always used cutesy names when talking to me, and sometimes my dad did too, but despite my crappy boyfriend in high school, I'd never had a man use terms of endearment on me.

I glanced around the building. We had hit a bit of an unexpected busy time. There were several customers wandering about. By now, the soothing holiday tunes on the speaker were nearly drowned out by all the chatter in the building.

"I guess it wouldn't hurt," I muttered to Patrick.

We worked well together, handing each other paper or tape when we needed it. And the line of six people grew exponentially before it dwindled back down.

When I sent off the last customer with a plaid wrapped box with a pinecone and cinnamon stick attached, I nearly collapsed into Patrick with relief.

He patted me on the back. "Wow. That was a rush," he said. "Who knew this little bookstore had this kind of traffic?"

I laughed. "I'm so glad you showed up. I would have drowned in all of these people if it weren't for you."

Patrick just smiled down at me. "Hey, maybe I should pick up a side gig here."

I squinted my eyes at him. "Are you trying to jack my job?"

He leaned over close to my ear and whispered. "Aren't you working for the school soon?"

I whispered back. "Yes, but I'll still be here part time, so please don't steal my job."

He wrinkled his nose at me. It was cute, and I found myself wanting to lean nearer to him.

"What the–?" an eerily familiar voice said.

Instinctively, I jerked away from Patrick. We were at my place of work anyway, and I didn't want to lose my professionalism. I twisted around to face Emily. She was scowling and breathing hard.

"I wondered why you were in here so long!" she shouted. She was looking at me, but it was clear who her words were directed at.

"Did you follow him?" I asked her. "Again?"

She ignored me, this time switching her target. "How dare you! I told you what would happen if you kept traipsing around with her!"

I glanced back at Patrick. Aside from the night we volunteered in the park, I hadn't seen the two of them together. It was strange to see how Patrick's face had turned stone cold and placid. His eyes darkened, and I could see his teeth clenching together.

"Emily. We're not going to do this here," he said languidly.

"And YOU," she yelled, pointing at me and then slamming her hands into the counter in front of me. "I warned you too."

I wasn't necessarily afraid of being harmed physically, but I was caught off guard by her explosiveness. I stepped back just as Patrick swam his arm around me, pressing gently into my stomach and pushing me behind him.

"Emily, you need to leave. This is too far, even for you," he said coolly.

I stared up at his back, a great protective wall before me.

Emily was yelling quite loudly this time, causing more of a scene than the time before. I glanced around to see if anyone had taken notice, and lo and behold my manager was charging in my direction with the team leader in tow. She looked mad, and I was worried that I'd get in trouble for causing a scene or at least for letting a non-employee work with me.

My manager and the owner of the store, Sandra, stopped abruptly next to Emily. She flicked her eyes to me. She seemed really mad. My stomach churned nervously.

"Ma'am, you're going to have to leave," she said.

Suddenly I forgot how to breathe. I was relieved, but also not–it was a strange feeling. I'd been certain she was going to yell at me first.

"Excuse me," Emily asked with her self-entitled tone. "She's the one who—"

"I already know who you are," Sandra said firmly. "I was told by my staff members about your behavior not too long ago."

I glanced up to see Patrick's expression, but he was still stern and cold.

"Hah!" Emily said. "I'm a paying customer!"

Patrick shook his head in disbelief. "Where's your purchase then?" he asked in a monotone voice. I didn't think that he was capable of that kind of lifelessness. I was so certain he attacked every situation with his go-get-em attitude and perseverance. But then again, I probably didn't know everything about him.

"I haven't found it yet," she spat back at him.

Sandra crossed her arms. "And you're not going to," she said. "I can't have you causing scenes in my building anymore. You need to go now."

"Just go," Patrick said through his teeth. He looked really mad too.

I couldn't imagine how it must feel to have someone cling onto you obsessively and follow you around and constantly threaten you.

Emily stood there in stubborn silence for a moment. When Sandra moved to grab hold of her and force her out, Emily jumped back and huffed. "Fine! I'll go. Jeez."

Sandra followed her to the door, but when they were only halfway, Emily turned around and shouted. "Remember! If he doesn't come back to me, my daddy will ruin him." Sandra placed her hand on Emily's back and sped up the process of escorting her outside.

I placed my hand on his arm. He turned and looked down at me, his expression turning sour then sad. "I'm so sorry," he said. "Just when I think she's done, she comes back. She shouldn't have come here. I'm so sorry."

I shook my head. "Patrick, it's fine. Or, it's not. But what I mean is it's not your fault. Okay? She's the crazy one. She's the one who can't take a hint. You're just trying to move on. And now that I—"

"Don't," Patrick said, cutting me off. "Don't you dare blame yourself for anything. Neither of us did anything wrong. We're okay. Okay?"

I nodded, but I wasn't sure it was true. As much as I wanted to keep hanging out with Patrick, it seemed like he had some things to sort out, and I was only making it more difficult. And if I was truly to get between him and his business, even if it was that little snake's ploy, I wouldn't be able to forgive myself.

I'd learned how he went to trade school and started his own business pretty much right out of the gate. He had to get a loan while he got started, and it was rough going for a while. But he worked through it. He was still working independently, but he had dreams of doing more, of having his own business. If Emily's father really did ruin him all because he was seeing me, then I knew I wouldn't be able to forgive myself for letting that happen.

It couldn't be my fault he lost his business. He was becoming more successful and needed the income for himself and for his aunt. I couldn't get in the way, even inadvertently.

I thought maybe I should stop seeing him for his own good.

CHAPTER 16

Patrick

IT HAD BEEN a few days since Emily's embarrassing scene in the bookstore. Every time I saw her, her behavior got uglier and greener and more obsessive. I just couldn't believe I had ever thought she was a good person and the right woman for me. I was angry at myself for being so blind for so long.

Not only was it taxing and annoying for me, but now it was affecting other people I cared about, too, like Holly, for instance. She hadn't called me and she wasn't answering my text messages. I didn't want to suffocate her with pressure to be around me after that ordeal, but I was worried that she was slipping away.

We were getting along so well. She was so kind and lovely. And while I once thought the same about Emily, I felt I was grown enough now to be a better judge of character. At least I hoped I was. I wondered if I should talk to Andrew about it. He had met her that night we volunteered at the park. Maybe he could confirm that she was just as sweet as I thought.

And if she was everything I thought she was, then it would be a real shame for Emily to run her off. But Emily was such a handful. Even after a year of telling her to let go and move on, she was still so desperate to cling to our relationship. I still didn't understand why, but it was becoming clearer that she couldn't be reasoned with.

Unfortunately, I thought there might be only one solution to her nonsense. I had to go to the people who had been dealing with her since she was born.

I walked through my house, which was entirely too quiet for comfort, and tugged on my boots. It was probably better to go then than wait any longer. I pulled on my wool-lined coat and eyed the scarf that Holly had hung around my neck the night of our walk. I had meant to give it back to her when I visited her at work. I had a whole plan for that day. I was going to surprise her at work, take her to lunch, give it back to her, and maybe, if the timing and the feelings were right, I might have kissed her like I didn't do that night in the city center park.

But then she had been so busy, and Emily had come and ruined the mood. And now, I didn't know what was going on with Holly. Maybe she'd already completely turned away from me.

Regardless of what Holly had decided, I needed to stand up to Emily once and for all.

It was a particularly brisk night with ice in the forecast, but I wanted to go out. I needed to talk to Emily's parents as soon as possible.

I started to head out the door, but I thought twice about the scarf. Maybe I needed to buck up and take it to her anyway. If anything, it belonged to her and she deserved to have it back. I could do that at least. I bundled the scarf in my hand and stepped outside.

The wind whistled softly through the trees, but it stung my nose and ears. This was the kind of cold I hated. It was dry and sucked the life out of me. I preferred the crisp chilly days with the promise of snow and those beautiful paper white fields.

As soon as I approached my truck, Emily's car came flying into my driveway, blocking my truck in. I huffed. I didn't know how she always knew when I was going to push her away even harder, because every time I was ready to try, she'd come to me with excuses or reasons to stay.

"Where you going, cowboy?" she asked me casually.

I hated it when she called me that.

"You mean you don't already know?" I said sarcastically. "I was under the impression you knew my schedule better than I do."

She gave a light and airy chuckle. Maybe a part of her was light-hearted. Maybe she wasn't all obsession and angst and drama. But even if that was true, it wasn't going to change my mind. I was done.

She glanced down at her phone and typed a short message before sliding it in her pocket and waltzing up to me.

"You have been throwing me off lately," she said. "But regardless of what you think, I don't follow you ALL of the time."

The fact that she could casually admit that she followed me at all told me that she wasn't getting the important message here. I wasn't the kind of person to be needlessly rude to anyone, but I wasn't afraid to be blunt.

"You shouldn't be following me at all," I said. "It's unsettling, and it's the last way you could ever get me back."

Emily laughed. "Oh, honey. I'm not trying to hurt you or scare you. I'm just making sure you don't do anything you'll regret."

I scoffed. "I've done enough regretting my decisions. I'm not going to make any more mistakes."

Her cutesy smile faltered but she shook it off. "Well, you just seem a little lost is all." She took another step toward me.

I took a step away. "I've never seen nor thought more clearly," I said. "I'm doing fine without you."

Emily donned a sad puppy face. "But Patty, I just miss you so much. I always regretted how things ended. And, now, seeing you with someone else...."

She reached up and toyed with the frayed edges of Holly's scarf in my hand. I pulled it away from her. "You don't get to be upset about that. Relationships happen with two people, Emily. At this point, ours is one-sided. It's obsolete."

"Patty, you don't mean that," she said, stepping up and grabbing the scarf in her hand. "You don't love her. You love me, remember?"

I shook my head. My words were falling on deaf ears. "Forget this," I said, turning.

But Emily yanked on the scarf, pulling it out of my hand and knocking me off my balance. She used my moment of vulnerability to spring up and grab the collar of my jacket, the tail of the scarf dragging in the snow.

I didn't have a second to react. She quickly put her arms around me in a bear hug. As soon as I got my bearings, I grabbed her arms and pushed her away from me. I saw a car go by.

"What are you doing?" I shouted, stepping away.

Emily smiled crookedly. "I thought I could just remind you of how we used to be," she said.

"Exactly!" I said. "USED TO be. We're not together anymore. And we never will be again."

I jerked the scarf out of her hands and wiped the snow off of the bottom.

"I'm sorry," she said, playing to her tender girlish side. "I was just shocked by our breakup. I just want us to be together again."

I wasn't going to deal with her repetitive lines. She'd overused them. They didn't affect me like they had the first couple of months.

"And stop doing crazy stuff like this! It's been a whole year. You should be over it by now. Everyone in this town is going to get the wrong idea about me if you can't leave me alone," I said, stomping away.

Emily stood there watching me leave, for once, speechless.

I turned around to face her one last time. "And please leave Holly alone. You're not to show up at her workplace or harass her in any way."

She put on a pouty face and whined another "I'm sorry. I won't do it again."

I didn't believe a word out of her mouth, so I continued on my intended journey. I got into my truck and pulled up enough to back up around her car. I left her standing in my yard with a blank expression.

Emily's parents' house wasn't far. Pam and Glen lived out on the edge of town in a large house with about one hundred acres surrounding them. They were well-off because Glen was a smart businessman and Pam was a doctor. They were good people, but I wondered if it wasn't their work ethic that helped bring out this side of their daughter that none of us wanted to see. They were both busy people without much time to deal with her problems.

I half-expected Emily to pull into the driveway right behind me, but thankfully, I arrived at the Norwood home on my own. I parked my truck and walked through the crunchy snow up to the big screened-in porch. I rang the doorbell and waited.

Pretty soon Pam answered the door. She seemed shocked to see me—rightfully so. I hadn't spoken to them in a few months. But I had developed a close relationship with them while I dated Emily. Even now, I felt like I loved and trusted them more than I ever had with her. They were just like an aunt and uncle set the way they took care of me.

"Patrick. I'm so surprised to see you. Is everything okay?" she asked, waving me in.

I took off my boots by the door per their 'clean household' rules. "Hi, Pam. Sorry to drop by unannounced like this."

She waved me off. "Oh, please. You know you can stop by any time. I wish I saw you more often, but I understand why I don't."

I followed her into the entertainment room, which had a big loop of chairs and couches with a couple of coffee tables in the middle. They used this room for house parties and important business meetings. This kind of felt like a business meeting, actually, just not the good kind.

"Glen! Come here! Patrick's visiting!" Pam called out.

I heard Glen's voice far off. He sounded happy to see me, and that made my heart lift a little. Then I remembered why I had come here to speak to them in the first place. Pretty soon, Glen shuffled in wearing his house slippers and a robe.

"Oh, dear," Pam said. "You could have taken the time to get properly dressed first."

Glen just laughed and came over to me. He gave me a friendly pat on the back and told me to sit. I sat at one end of the sofa while the other two sat on the far end.

"What's going on, son?" Glen asked.

"You look serious," Pam added.

I sighed. "It's a bit of a tough subject," I said, feeling pressure. I nervously rubbed the back of my neck.

"Do you need money?" Glen asked.

Pam swatted his leg while I just laughed it off awkwardly. "No, no, that's not it."

Pam waited expectantly while I searched for the words.

"Actually, uh, it's about Emily," I started.

Glen huffed. "You're not getting back together are you?" he said. "I did not like the way our girl treated you. I hate to say this as her father, but she was rather controlling of you. You're a good man! You don't deserve that at all!"

I gave a small smile. "No, we're not getting back together. But, uh, she does seem rather insistent on trying to get me to reconsider. She has been...." Man, I really didn't want to tell these two precious people that their daughter was crazy.

"Just be frank," Pam said.

I nodded. "Right. Well, she's been following me, apparently. She had been popping up once in a while trying to convince me that we should get back together, but now it's gone even farther."

Glen pressed his lips together and began to thumb his mustache. "Can you explain? What exactly is she doing now?"

I ruffled my hair. It was harder to report Emily's behavior than I thought it would be, even after she'd stopped at my house just now and forced herself on me. "Like I said, she had been popping up randomly, usually while I was at home, to pester me about getting back together. I've been telling her for months and months that I didn't think it was a good idea, that I didn't want to. And now... I've been kind of seeing someone. Well, I met a woman at the Santa Claus

Ball and then I…. Well anyway, I've been out with this woman a couple of times, and Emily followed us. She knows where we were and what we did."

Pam covered her mouth and closed her eyes.

"Well, she has now been to this woman's workplace and harassed her two times now. I was there the last time. I saw her get escorted out of the place. And today, well, today Emily showed up at my house again. She's saying the same things. She doesn't seem to understand the lines she's crossing. I just don't know what to do about her anymore. It's one thing to harass me, but to go after a woman I like–I can't have that."

Pam reached out and patted my knee. "I'm so sorry," she said.

CHAPTER 17

Holly

I FELT bad for being curious. I had decided it wasn't my place, that it was better if I just left Patrick alone. But when I got a text message from a random number saying that Emily and Patrick were together in front of his house, my curiosity got the best of me. *Were they fighting? Were they ending it for real? Could I possibly stop ignoring him and get back to hanging out with him like I really wanted?*

It was such a shame. I really wanted the best for Patrick. While I knew Emily's problems had nothing to do with me, I could tell my involvement was just making things worse. I figured it would be better for everyone to get over this if I would just step back for a while. And then maybe later on–just maybe–I could start seeing him again when she had finally stopped.

So I tugged on a sweater and a hat and slipped on my boots. I found Abigail standing in the kitchen, snacking on a bag of chips.

"Abbi," I said.

She almost jumped out of her socks, flinging a few chips across the small kitchen island.

"Holy granola, girl!" she yelled. "I thought you were still moping in your room! You scared me!"

I helped her sweep the fallen chips up and throw them into the trash can. "Can you help me with something?"

Before she could answer, Gretchen busted in through the front door. "He did it! He did it!" she said, rushing over to us with her arm stuck out.

Abigail and I stared at each other.

"Well!" Gretchen shouted excitedly. "Aren't you excited for me?!"

I finally cracked a smile. She had been waiting for so long for this moment. And it was finally here.

Abigail walked over and took Gretchen's hand to inspect her new engagement ring. I took a peek at it too. It was big and beautiful and flashy, just like Gretchen. It was perfect for her.

"How'd he pop the question?" Abigail asked.

For once, Gretchen didn't talk endlessly. She just smiled and told us that he'd simply just made her a nice dinner and given her the ring over dessert. They just spent the right of the night talking about wedding plans and just snuggling on the couch.

I thought it was great that he'd done something unexpectedly simple. All this time she was hoping for something extravagant and showy, but that wasn't what she needed at all. She just needed to be asked. She just needed the opportunity to say yes.

"Why'd you wait until now to tell us?" Abigail asked next.

Gretchen waved her off. "I hate to break it to you, but I told my sister first then I told my parents this morning. And now I'm here."

"Third on the list. Sweet," Abbi said.

I laughed and gave Gretchen a big hug. "This is great. Congratulations."

"Now," Abigail said, turning back to me. "What did you need help with?"

I thought about the text. I'd gotten it a few minutes ago. It was likely it was either a hoax or they'd moved on by now. "Oh. I don't think now is—"

"Don't be ridiculous," Gretchen said. "I'm exhausted by my own high. Let's do your thing."

I sighed. "Alright then...."

I explained the story briefly.

"We're going to go see what's up," Abigail insisted.

I nodded, still not sure whether I wanted to go, but Abbi pulling me out the door with Gretchen as backup didn't leave me much of a choice. We crawled into Gretchen's car, and I explained the way to Patrick's house. When we reached his street, she slowed slightly. I slid down slightly in the seat and peeked through the window, just in time to see Emily grab Patrick and give him a huge hug.

I looked away and laughed dryly to myself.

Gretchen turned to me and placed her hand on my leg. "Is that–?"

I nodded.

Even Abigail was quiet, though she always had something smart to say. She reached around from the back seat and held my hand.

I wished that I wasn't crying. It made me feel weak. I thought I was doing what was best for him, but maybe he didn't know what was best for him. I didn't know him THAT well after all. Maybe he was the kind of good guy who just made bad decisions about women.

Either way, it hurt. My heart squeezed painfully and my throat locked up. And at the same time, I was furious. All he'd done and said to get her away from him, and suddenly they were hugging in his driveway.

Even though Patrick and I weren't official boyfriend and girlfriend or anything, we'd spent all that time together the last couple of weeks. He'd told me about his family, he shared his experiences with me, he visited me at work and made me feel special, we laughed, we cried, and we'd nearly kissed that night.

Did all of those things we'd done together mean absolutely nothing to him? They meant something to me.

Eventually, we pulled into my driveway.

"Hey, wanna go watch some Christmas movies at my place?" Gretchen asked. "I have that big projector that you love."

I sniffled, feeling ridiculous for crying but appreciating my good company.

"I'll go get Carol," Abigail said.

She went in and collected a bag of goodies and blankets and brought them out along with Carol. She opened the front door so Carol could hop up into my lap.

She was excited to see me, even though we'd barely been gone for ten minutes. As I petted her, I realized just how close Patrick had been to me this whole time. His house was just a few streets away from mine.

Carol was dressed in her little Santa costume, and the bell on her collar jingled as she put her paws on my chest and licked at my face. I stroked her wiry coat until she calmed and laid down in my lap.

The rest of the car ride to Gretchen's house was quiet.

When we got there, we got some snacks together and settled in on the couch, me in the middle and my two best friends on either side. Carol lay on the floor in front of me. We chose an array of Christmas movies, from the classics to some of the newer ones that seemed sure to become classics. Abigail banned me from watching *White Christmas*. I wasn't mad about it. I'd watched it too many times the last time I was upset about a guy.

For about twenty minutes, everything was fine. We were watching *A Charlie Brown Christmas* and singing along with the songs. But my mind quickly returned to its track of anger about that night's situation.

"I just don't understand," I said.

Gretchen began, "You see, he's going to pick the small tree because—"

"Not that!" Abigail said, throwing an M&M at her. "Just wait for the rest."

Abigail was quick witted and observational. It probably had something to do with her forever half-finished major in psychology. She just seemed to catch on quicker than others. Or maybe she'd just grown to know me too well.

"Don't you think it's weird that we drove by right at the exact time?" I said.

It had crossed my mind that the timing was too perfect, but also I couldn't deny that they were in each other's arms he seemed to be letting it happen, though I couldn't remember seeing his arms at all, come to think of it.

"I thought that too," Gretchen said. "It was a bit odd."

Abigail squeezed the plush red pillow in her arms. "I think she set you up."

Gretchen cocked her head. "What do you mean?"

"You think she sent the text to me?" I wondered. "I wouldn't put it past her."

"She seems like a real piece of work from what you've told us so far," Gretchen said. "But I'd never even seen the girl until now."

Abigail hummed. "I think it's likely. She probably wanted you to see them together."

I sighed. "I've already pretty much stopped talking to him. I didn't want to totally freeze him out because he doesn't deserve it, but…. He's a smart guy. I'm sure he's started to get the hint."

Gretchen pouted. "That makes me sad," she said. "I only met him once, but I liked the guy. You two seemed to be getting along well based on your stories and all the cute things he did for you."

I thought about my graduation party and the date and his visit to the bookstore. "I don't know. The two of them were together for like, three years or something crazy like that. Maybe he just wanted to go back to her because it's easy."

Abigail frowned like she didn't believe me. I wasn't sure I believed myself. But it was the easiest explanation.

"Maybe you should go ahead and talk to him and get the whole story," Gretchen said.

I hoped that Abigail would disagree and take my side. She actually nodded her head in agreement, though she didn't verbalize it.

"What if it was a goodbye hug?" Gretchen said.

I wrinkled my nose. I didn't like the thought of that. And I didn't think that Patrick would be the type to go totally one-eighty. The day

Emily came to the bookstore and made a scene in front of both of us, he'd looked at her with such anger and frustration, and now they were together in his front yard. It did seem strange, and the timing did seem too on the nose. But whatever the reason behind it, it still happened, and it still bugged me.

Not only that, but it gave me a stronger reason to stay away from him. So I told myself that I would keep keeping my distance. I would let him do his thing and deal with Emily however he saw fit.

I tried my best to get back into the movie. I hardly laughed during *Christmas Vacation*, and even *Home Alone* wasn't keeping my mind from wandering to Patrick.

I couldn't deny that I was disappointed. I had begun having high hopes that something would happen between us, and the velvet-suited mystery man's kiss seemed to be going farther and farther into the back of my mind.

My mind ran in circles as we binge-watched Christmas movies and ordered a pizza and made a special chocolate-drizzled popcorn snack. Carol came up to sit with me, and I wrapped her up in my arms like a baby. She loved the attention, and I felt bad for not having spent as much time with her the last few weeks. I apologized in her floppy little ears for being distracted and promised that we'd go to the dog park the next morning.

CHAPTER 18

Patrick

I WAS STARTING to get particularly worried. It had been a full week since I heard anything substantial from Holly. I messaged her every day at least once, but the most I had heard back since Emily came to her workplace was that she was too busy to meet or check her phone often. I didn't quite believe it, but I gave her some space anyway. Something about the situation had caused her to pull away, not that I could blame her.

But I maintained a little bit of hope. There was a kids' Christmas craft event that we had talked about. We both had already planned to go to it, and I hoped I would see her there. Maybe I could get her to talk to me or at least listen.

I had spoken to Emily's parents and I was sure they were on my side. I knew if Holly would only give me a little bit more time, I could get rid of Emily and we could pick up right where we left off. I could seal that kiss that got interrupted. I could return her scarf and tell her I thought she was beautiful and amazing and that I liked her.

All I had to do was find her in person.

I laughed dryly to myself. The last time I was on the hunt for a woman, I wasn't successful, though, in that instance, I didn't have anything to go off of aside from the little green pin she wore and the way her arms tightened around me right before our kiss. And that sensation was becoming fainter and fainter the more time I spent with Holly. I still wondered about the mysterious woman from the Mistletoe Match, but now I was more concerned with Holly.

On the day of the kids' Christmas craft event at the church, I wore my best casual clothes—with help from Andrew—and I wore Holly's scarf so I could return it to her. I rehearsed what I'd say to her, how I'd explain the situation with Emily and how I'd sought help from her parents. I was going to tell her I wanted to keep seeing her, maybe dating her, if she was okay with it.

I was stationed at the table with the three year olds, and I thought about how Holly might have been better suited for the younger kids. She had a certain nurturing aura that I thought the kids would react well to, while I was easy going but big and perhaps too playful. I glanced around the room, hoping to see Holly at any of the other tables. But I didn't catch sight of her.

For a while, I thought that I just didn't see her in the chaos of making ornaments with the three year olds. But when I didn't see her twenty minutes in, roaming around the room under the guise of borrowing materials from the other tables, I knew that she hadn't come. I couldn't believe that she wasn't there. And my chest ached at the thought that she might be avoiding this place because of me. She'd showed me her list of events that she had planned to attend, so I knew she was super into the holiday spirit and she wanted to do as much as possible. So, it was wild that she'd abandoned this one.

I did my best to help out the three-year-old kids, but I wasn't good at it. I eventually got moved to the eight-year-old table, and it felt more manageable to me, but I couldn't have as much fun as usual. Of course, I did my best to appear happy for them, but inside I was really upset.

I felt like a little bit of *my* Christmas spirit had fizzled out.

After the ornament-making, I drove straight to my aunt's house. I had promised her that I'd come to help her out with a project she'd been unable to finish, something wood-working related. She was always doing crafty things like that after her job. She once said she dreamed of building cute little yard ornaments and interior decorations. She never got to do much of that, but she did her best to make the most of it now.

I wasn't sure what kind of project she needed my help with this time around, but I wanted to see her anyway. Now that I'd officially moved out on my own and didn't have to depend on her so much, I didn't see her often enough.

When I arrived at her little house on the west edge of town, I could hear her in her garage sanding away at something. I rapped on the metal door to give her a heads up before I opened it. By the time the door was up, she'd placed her clear safety glasses on the top of her head and removed her ventilation mask. I always thought she looked effortlessly cool. From a young age, I'd looked up to her strengths. She was strong, smart, and independent.

But there were some drawbacks to her personality, too.

In fact, if it weren't for my parents' early deaths, I never would have gotten this close to her. My aunt Louise was the kind to love from a distance. It took a long time to feel close to her, and even in the past several years of living with her, she'd never given much physical affection. Regardless of that, I knew she cared for me in other ways.

"Hey, stranger!" she called, after she turned her ventilation fan off and the garage started to fall silent.

I waved at her. "What are you up to this time?" I asked.

She chuckled. "You know, same old same old, just doing crazy old lady stuff."

I rolled my eyes at her. She was so far from old. In fact, she was only twelve years older than me. When my parents died, they were in their early forties, while my aunt, who had to take me in as a senior in high school, was hardly thirty. She was my mom's sister and grew up estranged from her family just like my mom. I never knew my grandparents on that side, and it sounded like they were the kind of people I was better off never knowing.

So, with my dad's parents gone and my parents gone, she was the only family I had left. It was strange at first, because we weren't all that close, but over the last four years we'd developed a routine, and now that I was recently moved out of her house I kind of missed her. And I thought she missed me too sometimes. In fact, I wasn't sure she even needed me now, but I came anyway.

I scanned her work area. It was her own kind of organized mess. But I could tell she liked what she was doing with her free time. She had that sort of breathless exhilarated look on her face that I spotted when she finished projects.

"Well, that is it?" I asked. All I saw was a giant curved slab of wood.

She wiped off the particles of dust on her overalls and stood from her little barstool seat. "Can't you tell? It's going to be Santa's next big ride!"

I raised an eyebrow. "What's that supposed to mean?"

She dragged me over to the corner of the garage and showed me a stack of slabs of wood. The one on top looked similar to the one she'd been in the middle of working in. "These are the sides of the sleigh. The bottom and back and everything is in the pile too. I've just gotta get it all carved out, all of the intricate parts."

I smiled. "Sorry, but I don't think this is gonna be done in time for Santa to use." I teased her.

She elbowed me in the side. "It's for next year."

"What'd you need me for anyway?"

She sighed. "I don't necessarily need you today, but when it comes time, I wanted to see if you'd be willing to help me put all the pieces together. I don't need your muscles so much as your ability to hold something on one side while I secure it on the other."

I shook my head and clicked my teeth. "See, this is why you need to get a boyfriend."

"I have plenty of friends," she shot back. "A couple of the girls at church. Mrs. Henson, too! I don't need any of them to be boys to be happy."

I crossed my arms. "Well, if you had a boyfriend, you wouldn't have to bother me to help you. If you found the right guy he'd be more than willing."

"Am I really putting you out?" she asked, even though she knew she wasn't.

I just shrugged and let her think what she wanted to think.

"Besides," she said, taking off her gloves and smacking me in the back of the head. "Isn't it about time for you to get back out there? You've always been more desperate for love than I have. It makes more sense to talk about your problems than mine."

I wasn't sure if I wanted to tell her about Emily, let alone about Holly, oh, and the mystery woman from the Santa Claus Ball. If I told her all of that, I knew she'd probably tease me for being a playboy. I didn't think I was, and I didn't think she'd truly think that either, but....

"What is it?" she asked. "You're all deep in thought and broody all of a sudden."

Maybe it was okay to talk to her about it. It might be worth it to have her outside opinion. She never liked Emily, though, so I decided to keep the details regarding her vague so as not to get her riled up.

"There's a girl, right?" she guessed before I even started talking. She eyeballed me up and down. "I did notice that you look a little more spiffed up than usual."

There was no use in denying it. I nodded.

"So, tell me about her. What's got you so down?" she asked. She settled back onto her barstool and then stood up suddenly. "Wait, it's not Emily, right?"

I laughed awkwardly. "No. it's certainly not Emily."

She sighed a breath of relief and fell back onto her seat again. She signaled to the workbench and I took my seat.

"Her name is Holly," I began.

"Ooh, Christmassy, you like that."

I shot her a warning look. It dawned on me that our relationship might have been more like brother and sister than it was aunt and nephew. But whatever, it was worked for us.

"Fine," she said, raising her hands. She rested back against the counter. "I won't interrupt."

"Okay, well, I met her at the beginning of the month, so it hasn't been long, but she intrigued me from the start. She's quippy and funny and she loves Christmas maybe more than me. She's really kind and loves kids and when she smiles she radiates this energy that—"

"Okay, that's enough," Louise said, wearing a grimace. "Get past the goo and tell me the problem."

A little bit of heat creeped up the back of my neck. I hadn't meant to unload all that mushy stuff, especially to my aunt, but it just flew out of my mouth without thinking. "Things have been going well, I think," I continued. "We've met a few times, and I think I'd consider at least one of those outings an official date."

"Did you tell her it was a date?" Louise cut me off.

I rolled my eyes. So much for not interrupting. "Yes... after...."

She scoffed. "Classic chicken move. What did she say about that?"

"She just... referred to it as a date also."

Louise shrugged nonchalantly. "Alright, seems fine then. Go on."

I gave her a blank stare. She might have been the younger sister between her and my mom, but she was definitely older sister material. "Well, I was about to tell her that I liked her, but suddenly she stopped talking to me. I've been sending her a message every day for the last week with little to no response each time. It just feels like she's getting farther away now, and I don't understand why."

Louise pressed her lips together in a thin, doubtful line. "What happened? Really."

My leg began to bounce up and down nervously. "Emily, I guess."

Louise tossed her head back and let out a growl. "Ugh, that little.... What'd she do?"

"I guess she told Holly that she was my girlfriend and she always would be...."

"And?" Louise egged me on, knowing that there must have been more. There was always more where it concerned Emily.

I wasn't sure why I felt like protecting Emily from Louise's wrath. She certainly didn't deserve to be protected, at least in my opinion.

And I supposed it would be easier for Louise to share her true opinion if she knew all of the facts of the matter.

So I told her. I told her about following us on our date, about visiting Holly at her workplace and pretty much threatening her. I told her what Emily said about getting her daddy to ruin my job if I didn't go back to her. And I told her about the unwarranted and completely unwanted hug in my driveway.

By the time I had finished, Louise had clenched her hands together under her chin and her eyes were squeezed tight. It looked like she could have been praying. Maybe she was....

"Here's the deal," she finally said after a moment of gathering herself. "You *have* to get rid of that little rat once and for all. And as for Holly... it sounds like she's been incredibly patient through this whole ordeal, but you can't blame her if she doesn't want to deal with it. Heck, I wouldn't want to."

I nodded. "I know. And I don't... I just want—"

"It's clear what you want," Louise said, cutting me off once again. "And that's great. But that's not the most important thing right now. That's not what's going to solve this matter."

I listened intensively. Even though my aunt hadn't been married, she did seem to have a knack for relationship advice.

"The last thing she needs is to be pushed or pressured. You need to give her some space so she can figure out what *she* wants."

"But what if—"

Louise shot up her index finger to silence me. "But not too much space. You have to let her know you care. And one text message every day doesn't do that. You need to find a way, something special, to show her clearly how you feel. Then maybe she'll reach out to you when she's ready."

"What if she doesn't?" I asked.

Louise crossed her arms over her chest. "Then you deal with it," she said simply.

CHAPTER 19

Holly

THE MORNING WAS fresh with new-fallen snow. I wasn't due to go to work until ten o'clock, so I spent my morning drinking hot cocoa and trying to read. But I couldn't focus on the book, and my hot cocoa didn't taste as sweet as usual. I didn't even eat the whole first round of marshmallows. I hated to admit it, but I felt like my holiday spirit had been sucked dry.

Maybe occasionally in the past, I would feel this way for a day or two because I felt like the world was too far beyond repair, or because I'd had a fight with my roommate back at college. Maybe once I had a crisis trying to decide if what I was going to school for was really what I wanted to do. Of course, I got over all of those.

But this time, the nagging feeling of apathy was just hanging around far too long. Even Abigail was at a loss, and she was always the one to find a way to cheer me up.

I'd never been lovesick before, and I wondered if this might be what it was like. I knew I needed to get over it. It was my decision to step back from Patrick, but he'd so quickly gotten back with his ex. It sort of crushed me. I felt special, then I felt worthless. I felt hopeful, then I felt dread. I felt magic, then I felt the harsh reality of life. Not everything was awesome.

Carol was lying next to me with her snout resting on my leg. I stared down at her, wondering what she might tell me if she could speak. *Would she tell me to get over it? Would she tell me it was okay to cry? Would she tell me to get back at him?*

I didn't know. And none of those answers sounded like an answer to me.

I half-heartedly got dressed for work. We were supposed to be taking a holiday photo today, and I had a cute reindeer antler headband and a Christmas sweater picked out, but I wasn't excited to wear them. I tugged them on anyway along with a pair of jeans and some warm booties that Gretchen had gotten me for my birthday.

When I glanced in the mirror before I left, I felt like my eyes were dim. And I hated that I was so upset over a guy that I'd only known for a couple of weeks. That wasn't how I was supposed to be. I had never cared that much before. *So, why was this time different?*

There was a little Santa hat sticky note stuck to the door as I was leaving. It was from Abigail and it was a reminder of the Christmas caroling that I had planned before... well, before all of this. But after I'd decided to avoid Patrick, I had also decided to avoid most of my planned Christmas outings. I told her I didn't want to go caroling, but if she was on me about it this early in the morning, I wasn't sure I'd be getting out of it.

At the bookstore in the break room where we also locked away our bags, there was a big vase of flowers in the middle of the table with a cute bow tied on it. I smiled at them, thinking that they were so beautiful. They were white carnations with accents of red holly sticking about it. I took a sniff and got curious about who they belonged to. *Had the owner's husband gotten them for her?* But if so, they would probably be in her office.

I snooped around the vase for a letter, and I found a small envelope sticking in the middle.

"Holly?" I said aloud as I read it. *They were for me?*

I gulped. There was a small chance that they were from my parents, but….

I slipped the little card out of the white envelope and read it.

"Holly. I understand that you're busy, and that's okay. But I'd really love to see you. I hope that soon you can spare some time to see me. Until then, I'll be waiting. Patrick."

"Who's that from?" one of the other workers asked. "Is it that guy that was here last week? Are you guys an item?"

I gave an awkward smile but shrugged. "No, we're not together. I'm not sure what this is for, actually."

"Well," the worker sighed, "whoever it's from has good taste. It's so nice of them to send you flowers randomly. I would love that."

It was a nice thing, usually. Except I didn't feel excited that these flowers were for me. Instead I felt a little… irritated? Annoyed? Just upset.

How could he send these to me just a couple of days after I witnessed him and his girlfriend hugging in his driveway? He had told me that she was his ex, but then he went ahead and pursued her after everything. My mind ran in circles at the thought. I tried to understand it.

Could I really have had him pegged so wrong? Did he ever actually care for me, or was he just wasting time? Was he waiting for some big scene from Emily to show that she still wanted to be with him? Were they just the on-and-off type of couple?

There were so many questions, it was frustrating.

At first, I wanted to stay out of the situation because I didn't want to be responsible for him losing his hard-earned job. Then I thought that it'd be better for him to see her and sort it out than try to do anything about it. I just needed to stay away for a while. But I never imagined that he'd go back to her right away. I didn't understand it at all, and it irked me.

I guessed that I had to accept the fact that he was not what I expected. And sometimes that was what happened when you truly got to know somebody.

But I resented that I had gotten to know him, because now it just hurt. I wished that the velvet-suited man at the Santa Claus Ball had found me. I wished that I could have seen his face and gotten to know him instead. I wished that I hadn't gotten sidetracked by Patrick.

I wondered if it was too late to go back to looking for him. It would be better than avoiding Patrick. If I found him, I would get over Patrick and kick him out of my mind. Yeah… that was what I needed to do.

"WHAT'S THAT?" Abigail asked when I came in the door holding the vase of flowers Patrick had left me.

"It's nothing," I said, setting them down on the kitchen counter and leaving them immediately. I hadn't even wanted to bring them home, but everyone else at work guilted me into it. I was just going to leave them there for the weekend and pretend like I was sad when I came back and found them wilted and dried out.

Instead, I'd buckled them in the front seat of my car, because who wants a knocked-over plant in their seat or even their floorboard? That'd be a mess to clean up. And I'd brought them inside because I didn't want to litter them in my front yard. If I brought them in, they could be Abigail's problem.

I went back into my room with Carol and gave her a couple of little treats. She wagged her tail and jumped up and down when I asked her if she wanted to go for a walk, so I got her regular harness on her and found her leash.

"Don't forget about the caroling tonight. We need to leave in about an hour," she said. "Gretchen will be here in twenty minutes–or maybe thirty since she is who she is."

I looped the handle of Carol's leash over my wrist and shoved my hands deep into my coat pockets. "I don't think I'm going to go to that," I said.

I tried to sneak out of the door, but Abigail ran over and stuck her foot out so I couldn't open it. "Excuse me," she said. "Not to be too tough, but you gotta get your heart out of the dump and move on, girl. Get out and do the stuff you like to do!"

I gulped. I knew I needed to do that, but I just didn't feel the motivation to do it. "I just feel—"

"I don't care how you feel," Abigail said. "You're going. Once you're out, once you sing those first couple of songs, you'll remember all the things you love about Christmas. You'll feel the joy you always feel. You're just letting this situation block you out of it, but it's not that big. You've just got tunnel vision."

Every part of me knew that she was right. I wasn't the kind of person who got down and stayed down, especially not during the Christmas season. I didn't like that the situation with Patrick had put me out. I'd already missed out on at least five or six events and volunteer opportunities because I wasn't afraid to see him. Maybe it was time for me to get back to it anyway.

"What if he's there?" I asked with a sigh. If I was being honest with myself, I was more afraid that he'd still make me weak at the knees, and the anger I felt toward him would melt away. I was afraid I couldn't be strong as long as I was standing in front of him.

"Then you'll sing anyway," she said, "just like you do every other year."

I let out a long pent-up exhale. "You won't let me do anything stupid, right?"

Abigail hooked her arm over my shoulders. "I've got a mind as clear as crystal. Don't worry. I've got your back."

She tagged along as we walked Carol around the block. I was dreading going out just a little bit, but when Gretchen arrived with her fiancé and everyone else was so excited, I did my best to get back to my usual self, too.

And really, singing carols was in my top three favorite things to do during Christmas. There was just something about getting together with a bunch of other people from the neighborhood and making beautiful music together. We would sing about the joys of Christmas, about miracles and love and cheer. It would bring smiles to people's faces.

So we went. The four of us headed to the community center,

where the rest of the carolers were already picking up their sheet music and chatting with one another.

My heart dropped when I spotted him. I couldn't be surprised that he was there, but we weren't there for even a whole minute, and already Patrick's presence was a glowing beacon grabbing my attention.

I grabbed Abigail's hand like a scared middle schooler going through a haunted house. She peered around and caught sight of him too. He also seemed to notice me right away, but I turned my head before he could catch me in his gaze.

"Just keep me away from him for now," I told her. "Please."

Abigail just nodded her head. Our little group collected our sheet music and found a spot along the group of carolers. They kept me in the middle, between Abigail and Gretchen, and I let them steer me to and fro, trusting that they help me keep my distance from Patrick for as long as possible. I did my best to appear normal, to take part in the singing, but my heart wasn't in it. Frankly, neither was my mind. Because even though Abigail and Gretchen were trying to guard me, that didn't mean that Patrick couldn't sneak up and break down our defenses.

About the fourth stop on our caroling journey, Gretchen and Joey got separated from us because they got too caught up in each other's eyes or something ridiculous, which left my left side wide open. It was the perfect opportunity for Patrick to sneak in, and he did.

I was sure that he'd try to talk to me right away, but he just stood there and got ready for the next song. He held out his sheet music like a professional. I couldn't help but watch him out of the corner of my eye. And I noticed that he was wearing my scarf.

My heart did a little dance, though I wasn't sure about the feeling that matched it. I was getting sucked into my thoughts when the song started. Instead of singing along, I was immediately enraptured by Patrick's voice. It was rich and soulful and clear. He was a great singer. It made my heart sway a little.

I was even too distracted in trying not to look at him when he reached over and flipped over my sheet music. I hadn't even noticed that I was on the wrong page. He didn't say a word. He just flipped over the page, pointed to the right line, and kept singing.

He stuck next to me the rest of the night. Once I had looked up at Abigail, but she just shrugged at me. I was a little angry with her at failing to protect me. She had said she wouldn't let me do anything stupid, but the longer Patrick was by my side, the harder it was not to look at him and his familiar eyes, the harder it was not to get soaked up in his singing voice or enchanted by his wonderful scent.

As our caroling group continued from door to door getting donations for a local charity for animal shelters, I found myself starting to relax. In spite of all the things I'd thought or told myself, even though he hadn't even spoken to me yet, I had to admit that it felt good to be by his side again.

Still, I intended to leave as soon as we were done.

But at the end of the night, while Abigail and I were waiting for Gretchen and Joey to find us, Patrick finally faced me. He stood in front of me toe to toe and looked down intentionally at my face. I sensed some exchange between him and Abigail, and next thing I knew, Abigail was leaving me.

I was about to call after her when Patrick spoke my name.

"Holly," he said almost breathlessly. "Will you please look at me? I've been begging you to meet my eyes all night."

My heart aches for him at the sound of his voice. He sounded hurt, and I didn't like the idea that I had done that to him. Regardless of what I thought about his relationship with Emily, I still cared for him. I still wanted what was best for him.

I brought myself to meet his gray-blue eyes. They looked tired and sad, but there was a little spark far in the back that shone like the north star when he gave the faintest smile.

"There you are," he said.

His voice echoed somewhere deep in my soul, eliciting a tingle through my body. He reminded me of something just then....

"Holly," he said again. "Can we please talk for a moment? Will you finally speak to me?"

There was that ache in his voice again. It made me weak in the knees, just like I'd thought. But maybe he deserved an explanation. He had been trying to reach me, but I made myself unavailable and I never told him why.

Maybe if I just told him how I really felt now... we could both move on.

CHAPTER 20

Patrick

I almost couldn't contain my excitement as soon as I saw Holly. She looked lovely as ever with her long hair curled into waves. But her eyes looked a little duller than usual, more earthy and dry than like a bright emerald.

I wanted to go to her, but as soon as she saw me, she turned away. At that moment it felt like someone had gut-punched me. She definitely saw me, and she definitely ignored me, too. I remembered what my aunt Louise had told me about giving her space while still letting her know I cared and wanted to see her when she was ready. I supposed she got the flowers when she went to work, but maybe she didn't like them. Maybe she needed more time.

So throughout our caroling tour, I kept my eye on her. I tried to sneak in, but her friends had barricaded her off. I closed in after the first couple of songs, and when her friend on the left side got hung up chatting with her boyfriend about the archway in someone's yard, I used the moment to get next to her.

Holly sensed me there. I could tell by how stiff she became, but she didn't shoo me away. It still felt like she was crumbling up my heart like a used piece of paper, but I needed to tell her how I felt. I needed to get some kind of idea why she was pushing me away all of a sudden. So I stayed. I watched her from the corner of my eye.

It was kind of cute how she seemed unfocused on the music. She wasn't paying a lick of attention and she wasn't even on the right song. I took the liberty of gently sliding the sheet music out of her hand and flipping it over. I pointed to the line we were on.

But she never even looked at me. The rest of the night, she wouldn't meet my eyes. She wouldn't say a word. Finally, in the last few songs, she started to loosen up and sing a little. She had a sweet, pure voice that melted my heart a little.

When the night was over and it seemed like she was trying to leave without a word, I bravely stood my ground and spoke to her. I was surprised when she finally met my eyes. She seemed more sad than angry. But I was so relieved when she agreed to talk with me.

"Should we go on a short walk, then?" I asked her.

She glanced over her shoulder at her friends and nodded. "Okay," she said softly. It was the first real word out of her mouth.

Holly had her hands tucked deeply in the pockets of her coat. I had wanted to take hold of them and tell her what was going on in my heart, that she was all I could think about. But it wasn't time yet.

So, we just walked slowly. I wasn't sure if she felt the same way, but the night's atmosphere was romantic. With the other carolers dispersed it had grown quiet, and the further we walked away, the more peaceful the night became. The freshly fallen snow from the morning had covered the roofs of houses, but everyone's Christmas lights shone against it like a kaleidoscopic dream. Above the lights, the moon glared brightly.

"How did you like the caroling?" I asked, wanting to ease into conversation.

"It was nice," she said simply.

I sighed. I didn't know how to make her open up. "Between volunteering and caroling, which do you prefer?"

She was quiet for a moment, perhaps caught off guard by my random question. "I like caroling a lot," she finally said, "but I enjoy working with the kids more."

My heart raced even at such a simple sentence. But it was a whole sentence, so I knew she must have been warming up to me again.

"What was your favorite volunteer activity so far?" I asked.

She glanced up at me. Really it was like a quick flick of her eyes. But she looked at me. "Maybe the gingerbread house making event," she said sheepishly.

My heart rose again. "That was fun. Though I still feel like little Anthony should have won."

I saw the corner of her mouth twitch with a smile. "If only you'd followed the rules. It was a gingerbread house activity, not a gingerbread car activity."

I gave a short laugh. "Well, regardless, I liked it. But I think decorating the park was my favorite."

She hesitated in the silence before asking, "Why's that?"

I couldn't contain my smile. "Because that's where I met you."

For just a moment her smile grew, but then it crashed into a flat, sad line. This woman was breaking my heart. I wanted to understand what was going on with her. Even if it wasn't because of me, I just wanted to make sure she was okay.

"Holly," I said, gently taking hold of her arm and pulling us to a stop in the middle of the sidewalk. "Where have you been? I haven't seen you at all. And I was sure you'd be there at the ornament activity. I'm just worried. I thought you'd be there."

Holly hung her head. She didn't pull her arm out of my grasp, but she was back to looking sad and heavy hearted. She stared down at the ground. I wasn't sure if it was appropriate, but I hooked my finger under her chin and lifted it so she would meet my gaze. Something about the gesture seemed familiar, like I had done it before to her.

"Holly," I said, softly urging her to speak.

She pulled in her lips for a moment, pressing them together nervously. That seemed familiar too....

"Holly, please, just tell me what's wrong."

She let out a short sigh before locking her eyes onto mine. "Patrick, I can't be around you like this."

Her words stabbed at my heart.

"Not when you're back with Emily," she added.

I was confused. *Back with Emily? Had she been back there? Had she told her that we were together again?* "What do you mean? Did she say something to you?" I asked.

Holly drew her eyebrows together and tugged her face out of my hand. "I saw you two… in your driveway."

The realization was setting in.

"You were hugging her," Holly said. "I thought that we… I thought you like—"

"Oh, Holly," I said. I wanted to wrap her up in a hug–all of this distance because of some misunderstanding. "I'm so sorry. I wished you hadn't seen that."

She scoffed at me. "Right," she said, annoyed.

"But it's just a misunderstanding," I said quickly. "Yes. Emily hugged me. *She* hugged me. But it was totally unwarranted and of course, I didn't hug her back. I stepped away as soon as I could react. I was on my way to see you when she stopped by and… well… you saw what happened. But I didn't want that. We aren't together."

I slid my hand down her arm and pulled her hand out of her pocket, wrapping it in my hand.

"I've been desperate to see you," I told her. I felt like this was the moment to show her how I felt, that I didn't care at all about Emily and that I wanted her. "Holly, you've completely flooded my mind. I couldn't stop thinking about you. Every day, I felt you were pulling away from me. My heart felt like it was splitting into pieces. I don't want anything to do with Emily. I'm totally captivated by you."

Holly breathed in shallowly. I couldn't tell if she was relieved or if she didn't believe me.

Oh, how I wanted to kiss her… but not yet. It wasn't time yet.

It felt like eternity passed while I was waiting for her to respond. I gripped her hand a little tighter, and she squeezed back. "I believe you," she said.

I let out a sigh of relief and pulled her into a hug, wrapping my arms around her shoulders. She felt familiar. The only other woman I'd hugged like this was Emily, but she certainly wasn't Emily. All I knew was that Holly was in my arms and she believed me.

"I thought that she was going to come after you," Holly whispered into my shoulder. "I thought you were going to lose your business. So I thought maybe you went back to her so you could protect yourself... I thought—"

I pulled far enough away to look Holly in the face. I shook my head. "She doesn't have as much power as she thinks she has. She's just crafty with her words. But I'm so sorry you saw that. I wish it didn't happen. I wish you didn't happen to drive by."

Holly pressed back a little farther. "Actually, I drove by on purpose," she said.

My heart lifted. "You were coming to my house to see me?"

She shook her head. "Not exactly." She pulled out her phone from her back pocket and pulled up a message to show me. "I got a text from that night saying that you two were together. I was just curious... so I got my friends to drive me there."

It felt like someone dropped a mallet on my stomach. "Emily. She did this. That's her number." Unfortunately, I knew her number by heart. "I'm not sure how she got your number, but she is crafty and sly. She probably tricked someone into giving her your number or something."

Holly put her phone back in her pocket. "I thought the timing was too perfect," she said sadly. "And I really didn't want to believe you were that kind of guy. I mean, I know we weren't *together* together, but..."

I smiled down at her and cupped her cool cheek in my face. I wished I had brought her scarf back so I could loop it over her head and tell her that she was the one I wanted. But before I could make an even grander gesture, there was something I needed to take care of.

"Listen, Holly," I said. "I like you, and I would never do anything to hurt you. But Emily is just going to keep getting in the way. So, I've taken some steps to get her to leave both you and me alone for good."

Holly relaxed her face into my palm. "How are you going to do that?"

CHAPTER 21

Holly

A few days later, I felt a little strange, I had to admit, going to a diner with my love interest and his ex-girlfriend's parents. It felt like I had crossed some kind of line, but Patrick assured me that despite Emily's behavior, her parents were good people. We could trust them, and they might be our last bit of hope at getting her to leave us alone.

I let Patrick lead me by the hand into the restaurant. He laced his fingers naturally through mine, and I wondered if his heart wasn't going as crazy as I felt. He was so casual about it, but this was the first time we'd held hands like this.

And my heart was beating anxiously on top of that. We'd just made it to the table where Emily's parents were waiting for us. The two of them looked kind enough. The lady was probably nearing fifty, and she wore her hair short and dyed a mahogany red color. She donned a pair of bit pearl earrings on her ears and a matching pearl necklace around her neck. The man's hair was short and thinning, and he had a mustache and beard that were spotted with gray and white. He wore a nice plaid button-up shirt.

The two of them stood as Patrick and I neared the table. They first reached out to give Patrick a hug, which surprised me. I thought it would be more of a handshake situation. But apparently, they were closer than I thought. I suddenly felt a little bit jealous. I wondered if Patrick would have a good relationship with my parents.

"Patrick, it's so good to see you again," the woman said.

Patrick nodded and gave her a quick kiss on the cheek. "Thank you so much for meeting us. This is Holly," he said, gesturing to me.

I gave an awkward little wave and the two of them smiled at me.

"This is Glen and Pam," Patrick explained. "They're Emily's parents."

I nodded politely. "It's nice to meet you."

I felt so awkward. But Patrick was sure we needed them to get Emily off of our backs for good.

Glen gestured to us to sit down, so we sat on one side of the table while Emily's parents sat on the other side. "I want to apologize for all of the trouble our daughter has been putting you through," he said, looking deep into my eyes.

He seemed sincere. I was still a little skeptical, but maybe Patrick was right. It just seemed impossible for a little green monster like Emily to come from two saints.

"Oh, uh, thank you for saying that," I said. But I wasn't really sure what the proper response was supposed to be in this situation.

"So," Patrick began, "I already told you about most of our issues lately, how Emily is following us, and coming to our workplaces to threaten us and tell us not see each other."

Pam sighed and nodded her head. "I never imagined she'd go that far."

I gave her a tight smile, trying my best to look sympathetic rather than angry. But the truth was, I was angry. Emily was stirring up too much trouble. Everything would have been fine without her. But I couldn't exactly rag on her with her parents in front of us willing to help.

Patrick cleared his throat awkwardly. "You see, when I spoke to you, I didn't tell you every single detail."

Pam placed her arms on the table top and folded her fingers together. "What do you mean?"

Before he could answer, the waiter came over and asked for our drink orders. It was awkward to go back and forth between talking seriously and being nice to the waiter. But we all put in our drink orders and resumed.

Patrick seemed nervous, so I slid my hand under the table and patted him on the leg. He glanced first at me, then redirected his attention up at Glen, not wanting to deliver the next bit of news. But, as he'd said to me, he knew that it was the only sure way to convince them to intervene and do more than give Emily a stern talking to.

"There's more to the story," Patrick said.

Glen began stroking his mustache, leaning back into the cushion of the seat. "Go on, then."

Patrick took in a deep breath then released it. "Emily keeps telling Holly that if I don't go back to her or if Holly doesn't refuse to see me that you'll… ruin my business. All you have to do is say the word, and I'll be done for."

Glen froze. He stopped twirling his mustache and sat up straight in his chair.

"She said what now?" Pam asked, also sitting up straighter. "Surely not…." She looked at me, seemingly waiting for my response.

I was hoping to get through this meeting without having to do much talking, but it seemed like the spotlight was already on me. I nodded. "I'm sorry, but it's true. She told me that her father had power, so all she had to do was say the word and he'd—you'd be able to ruin his business."

Glen pinched his bushy eyebrows together tightly. "Surely you didn't believe that nonsense," he said to Patrick. "I would never do that!"

Patrick nodded. "I know you wouldn't, but, of course, Holly didn't know you, so she wasn't sure if that was true. She pretty much froze me out for the last week, actually," he said, giving me a teasing glare.

My cheeks flushed a bit. *Was this really the time to bring that up? Was this his idea of flirting, in front of his ex-girlfriend's parents, too?* I pinched his leg under the table, and he laughed.

Pam gave a small smile between the two of us. She seemed good-natured and caring. I could see it in her eyes when she looked at Patrick. Suddenly, I was aware of the closeness these three shared. I was happy then that Patrick had some kind of parental figure in his life after he lost his parents.

Meanwhile, Glen was growing angrier. He was about to say something, but our table was interrupted by the waiter again, bringing us our coffee and hot cocoa. We placed our food orders and sent the waiter away.

"This is just ridiculous," Glen grumbled. "I don't care who my daughter has a relationship with or who she broke up with. I don't care how it started or how it ended. I would never ruin someone for her, especially you, Patrick."

Pam reached over the table and patted his arm. "You've been like a son to us," she said. "We'd never hurt you."

Patrick nodded. "I know that. You're good people. I trust you."

Glen huffed, still bothered by the news. "You're sure that she said that?" he asked, glancing over at me. I knew they might not trust me. Considering they didn't know me and Patrick's bad track record with picking evil girlfriends, they might have been right to be suspicious of me.

"Just how do you expect us to help?" Pam asked. "I wouldn't feel right about hurting her either. I know what she's been doing is wrong, but... she is our daughter."

I sympathized with her then. I imagined it would be difficult to have a family member like that. You loved them, but you didn't want to see them in trouble.

"I don't want to hurt her either," I said. "We just wanted to be free from her pestering us. I want Patrick to be able to relax and not worry about her lurking around."

"I have a potential plan," Patrick explained. "I don't expect you to do any of this simply because I asked. I want you to hear it for yourself, so you know."

Glen crossed his arms. "And just how do you expect us to do that? She wouldn't say that with us around."

"That's why you'll have to be out of sight," Patrick said.

We talked through the plan a little bit. I really felt like I shouldn't be there at the time. But Patrick convinced me that he wanted me there. Just as he'd said, Glen and Pam did seem to be good people. They were hesitant at first, but soon they were supportive of the idea and said that they'd agree to help us out the best they could.

With the Emily subject over and our food delivered, we were able to change the topic to something less anxiety-inducing–Christmas.

"Christmas is only a few days away now. Just what are you planning to do?" Pam asked. She popped a piece of medium-rare steak in her mouth and waited for an answer.

I looked at Patrick for a response, but he looked at me and nodded. "Yes, please tell us what your plans are."

There he was again, teasing me. The whole past couple of days since we made up, he had been egging me on about ditching him or ignoring him. I promised that I wouldn't do that anymore, even if I saw him hugging some random girl again. I'd give him a piece of my mind right off the bat. Of course, he promised that that would never happen.

"I'm not sure exactly what to do. Maybe I'll go visit my parents," I said.

"Oh, that's lovely," Pam said. "Are they nearby?"

I nodded. "They live in Noel."

Patrick's head jerked over to me. Maybe that was some information he didn't know yet. He looked at me with a pinpoint gaze.

"And just what does your Christmas usually look like?" Glen asked. "Do you have any family traditions?"

I smiled. "Of course. They own a bakery, so they're always busy making cookies and things for other people. But we always spend the night before Christmas making cookies for ourselves. We watch Christmas movies and travel around looking at the lights throughout the town. It's a simple tradition, but I love it."

I felt Patrick's gaze staring into me. I wasn't quite sure what his expression meant. But on the off chance he was offended I hadn't mentioned him in my plans, I added an endnote.

"Maybe I'll have to include this guy somewhere in my plans," I said, knocking my knee into his. He grinned at me lopsidedly. "He just keeps popping up. I think it'd be easier to include him in my plans this time instead of leaving him be."

"Again," Patrick muttered before he took a drink.

We all chatted and laughed together for another hour before we parted ways from the restaurant. The couple said they hoped to see me again and that they wished us the best of luck. On the way out, I overheard some people talking about another event coming up soon. Every year on the day before Christmas Eve, there was a huge festival in the big park where Patrick and I had met for the first time. There would be little contests and live music and food and even a section made for ice skating.

I vowed right then that I would not miss any of that. I was going to take advantage of the few days we had leading up to Christmas.

As we exited the diner, Patrick headed for his truck, but I grabbed his hand and led him in the other direction. "Let's take a walk," I said.

He smiled and gave my hand a squeeze. I suddenly felt the spirit of Christmas coursing through my veins again.

CHAPTER 22

Patrick

"I HAVE to say I didn't expect you to call me," Emily said.

It hadn't been easy, but I had called her to meet, saying we could talk over dinner. I asked her to meet me at the place of our first date, a little retro diner with plastic booth seats and red barstools.

She showed up all dressed up like usual, her dark hair straightened so it fell just so over her shoulders and down her back. She wore red lipstick that drew attention to her full lips, and her eyes were winged with eyeliner that she thought made her look catty in all the right ways. She even wore a mini skirt, but at least she had enough sense to wear tights underneath. She was certainly trying to win me over with her looks.

I shrugged and gestured for her to sit on one side of the booth. I sat across from her and folded my hands together on top of the table. "I gave it a lot of thought, and I decided to take you seriously," I told her.

She smirked. "I thought you might have reconsidered since you decided to bring me to this place where we had our first date."

I forced a smile. I was just playing a part for now. But until I could prove to her parents that she'd said those terrible things, I needed to pretend that I liked her again.

"Well," I said, "you were very convincing."

She gave a little laugh and leaned across the table toward me. "Well, Patty, you were being so stubborn."

I ran my hand through my hair like I knew she liked. "I didn't realize you were still so… passionate."

Emily batted her eyes at me. "Baby, you had to know that I was still in love with you. I made it so obvious. I just don't understand why you were being so difficult."

I had to be careful with my words. I had to make sure that I was believable. But I didn't want to lie outright….

"I guess," I began thoughtfully, "that I wanted to see how much you really loved me. I didn't know how far you'd go."

She grinned evilly. "Oh, my, my," she said, crawling her fingers across the table and walking them up my hand and wrist. "Here I thought I was the clever one. But I guess you were testing me, too."

I laughed. "Sorry I made you chase me all over town," I said. "But now I know how much you love me."

She snaked her fingers around my wrist and pulled my hands toward her. "But, Patty," she whispered, "what I need to know is how much you love me. Don't I deserve to know after all of that trouble you put me through?"

I gritted my teeth and took her hand. It felt so cold and unfamiliar. It felt so uncomfortable. "Emily, I've just been having a hard time recently. I'm not sure what brought it on. I thought I needed a change, so I pushed you away so suddenly."

She put on her pouty face. "You said a lot of things that really hurt me," she said.

I sighed. "I'm sorry about that. I never meant to hurt you. I was just feeling overwhelmed with… work and stuff. And I've been thinking about my parents a lot."

It felt cheap to use them as an excuse. But it was true. Thinking about their relationship had made me question my own. Of course, there were probably sides to their marriage that I never got to see, and I never got to fully understand their connection before they died, but I knew that whatever I had with Emily was not it. Emily was controlling, whereas my mother was caring and let me and my father both be ourselves. Emily was nosy and manipulative, whereas my mother was kind and communicative.

And I wasn't playing the role of my father very well. I didn't communicate. I let Emily walk all over me. I didn't stand up for myself. I didn't value myself. My father was a confident and carefree man. I wanted to be like him, but I couldn't be that person by Emily's side. I deserved better.

"Oh, Patty, I wish you had let me take care of everything for you," she said. "You know I can do it. And with my parents' help, I can accomplish a lot. They have a lot of power, as you know."

Was this it? Was this the time for me to go for the gold?

"But you can make it up to me," Emily said quietly. She laced her fingers through mine and pulled my hands closer to her. She leaned over the table like she was going to kiss me. "C'mon, show me that you're sorry for pushing me away for so long."

It took everything in me not to push her away. Instead, I whispered in her ear. "Let's save it for later," I said, gesturing to the people on the other side of the diner. "Don't you think there's too many people here?"

She giggled and sat back down. I gently pulled my hands away and brought them back to my side. For good measure, I hid them under the table so she couldn't steal them away again.

We went ahead and ordered and I let her take my French fries like I used to. I wished she'd just get her own instead of ordering a salad and pretending like she couldn't afford the calories. I wondered what Holly would order if we were to go out again. I made a note to take her to a real dinner, just the two of us, after this whole mess was sorted out.

I barely touched my food, and instead got Emily talking about herself. She was very good at it. She told me about the shopping she had done and the times she had gone out with her friends.

"I would have had more fun if I didn't have to keep such a close eye on you," she told me.

I forced a laugh. "You were very impressive," I told her. "I was surprised by how determined you were to have me back."

She grinned. "Did you like that?"

I nodded because I couldn't bring myself to actually say yes. "How did you know what to do to get me back?"

"Oh, Patty, I know how much you love your little electric business. You take so much pride in it even though it's so small. I knew you wouldn't want to lose it," she said, stealing another French fry from my plate.

It was hard for me not to grimace at her little digs. *Did she think saying these things was cute?*

"So, did you ever talk to your parents about it?" I asked.

She leaned back in her seat. "Well, Daddy has been quite busy lately, so I didn't get around to it. But thankfully I didn't have to since you decided to come back to me."

I clenched my teeth. She was so shameless. I just wanted this to be over with already.

"What would you have done if I didn't come back to you?" I asked. I was genuinely curious to see how far she'd have gone.

Emily just laughed. "My Patty," she said, running the toe of her shoe against my calf. "I just couldn't stand the idea of you with another woman. And when I saw you kiss someone else at the Santa Claus Ball, I knew I had to act fast, so I did what I had to do. The farther you got from me, the more I wanted you. So I'll always do what I have to do to get you back."

The way she talked sent chills down my back. "That was you? You pulled the fire alarm during the Mistletoe Match?"

She shrugged coolly, like it was some impressive feat. "Well aren't you glad I did it?" she said with an expectant smile. "Because we're here now. You didn't have to waste any more of your time with some random woman. And Daddy didn't have to ruin your little business. I think it all worked out."

I was quivering from the inside out. *How could she be proud of that?*

How could she be boasting about anything she'd done? She truly didn't care about me at all. I was just some kind of possession to her. And not only did she threaten the one thing I'd built for myself, but she'd ruined my chances of meeting that mystery woman that night. Of course, I'd still met Holly, but she almost got in the way of that too.

I stood up from the booth.

"What's up, cowboy?" she said. Then a devilish grin creeped across her face. "Are you ready to leave so you can finally pay me back?"

My stomach twisted up in knots at the thought. "No," I said. "Actually, I don't think I can do this after all."

She pressed out of her seat angrily. "What does that mean?" she spat.

"I used to think you were beautiful and kind and smart, but you're not," I said. "You're just selfish and mean and superficial."

She all but growled as she got in my face again. "So that's it? You want me to be the bad guy? Is that what this is? I guess I'll have to talk to my daddy after all! Your stupid little light business will be done for by tomorrow!"

"You know what's done for?" Glen said, standing up from the booth behind Emily. "Your access to our money."

Emily spun around. "Daddy?" she said, cowering like a spurned dog. "I… I didn't mean–"

Pam stepped around her husband and grabbed her daughter's wrist. "C'mon," she said. "We're leaving this place. I don't know how you turned out to be like this, but your father's right. You're not getting another cent from us until you've learned your lesson."

Emily yanked out of her mother's grasp. "Mom! You can't do that… I need it."

Glen crossed his arms and huffed. "What you need is to learn what it means to have nothing. You need to learn to be kind, to share, and to accept that you can't get everything you want."

I'd never seen either of Emily's parents so angry before. Pam's face was so red, and the crease between Glen's eyebrows was canyon deep.

"I'll set you up with one of my companies out of state," Glen said. "You'll work for a living, and you'll learn your lesson soon enough."

He moved to capture her arm again, but she sprung at me like I'd save her. I dodged her and waved for Holly to come out. She slid out of the same booth where Glen and Pam had been sitting. When Emily spotted her, she first looked furious, but her fire fizzled out.

"You were all working against me this whole time?" she asked, defeated.

I almost felt sympathetic. I took Holly's hand in mine and gave Emily one last stern look. "You've been doing this to yourself," I told her. "It's time for all of us to move on from this. I hope you can grow up and have a good life apart from me."

As I brushed past her with Holly in tow, I heard her mutter that she'd agree to go. "Fine, I'll go as long as I can keep my clothes and my car," she said. "They're worth more to me than him anyway."

I let out a long, pent-up sigh. She always had to have the last word. But that was her problem. I was looking ahead to much better things.

CHAPTER 23

Holly

THE LAST FEW days had been a wild ride. But Glen and Pam confirmed that Emily was officially sent off to work at one of their companies on the coast. I was relieved, but the biggest weight was lifted off Patrick.

He was like a whole new man. When I first met him, I thought he was lighthearted and cool and kind, but now, he was even more so. And those times he'd been a little flirty with me were just the tip of the iceberg. The man was the definition of suave. But mostly, it was the light in his eyes that shined the brightest. The blue in them became iceberg-clear. It was like a mirror of peace and happiness when I looked into them. I caught myself slipping into them again and again.

After the Emily ordeal, we'd had a couple of days of work to put under our belts, but it was officially the day before Christmas Eve, and it was time for the biggest festival of the whole season. It was even grander than the Santa Claus Ball. Instead of being localized at the auditorium, the party was spread throughout the whole center of the town, with Yule Park being the epicenter.

"This is my favorite place during Christmas," I told Patrick as we strolled through the park. It was totally decked out, bigger and brighter than the Santa Claus Ball. There were some repeat decorations, like the sleigh and the live reindeer, but now, rather than aiming for elegance, it was all about the fun.

There were all kinds of games for kids—and adults who felt young —to play, tossing the ring on the antlers or bobbing for apples in the cold water. I never totally understood why the kids liked that one so much, but maybe it was the thrill of the chill of the ice on their faces that shot adrenaline through them. Then there was an area for more traditional games like Fly, Feather, Fly, which involved the kids keeping a little fluff of cotton afloat in the air for as long as possible using only their breath. And there was a special scavenger hunt in which anyone could find certain prizes hidden throughout the city.

"Have you ever participated in the scavenger hunt?" I asked Patrick.

He laughed and puffed up his chest. "Please, the Professional at Fun basically invented scavenger hunts."

"So you can help us win something, then?" I asked.

He booped me on the nose with his finger. "We can win all the things," he said, squinting his eyes.

He did a cute little thing where he arched one eyebrow and wiggled it a little. It was endearing to me, but I couldn't let him know it. So I just pressed my lips together. "C'mon, you're starting to sound like Emily. Let's not be greedy and just aim for one thing."

"How about two?" he said. It was more of a statement than a question, but he'd said it with an adorable lilt in his voice, so it made me crack a smile.

"Fine, two it is," I said.

So to start off our day, we searched for the best prize. It was a coupon for a spa date in one of the cabins a couple of towns over. It included a free day trip up to the mountain cabin, a massage, a hot tub, a romantic dinner, and free ski rentals.

"We're gonna have the most fun date ever," he said. It was cute how determined he was to win.

And thanks to me and my genius knowledge of all things Christmas and books, I was able to help us decode a passage from *A Christmas Carol*. Patrick recalled that it had been showing at the auditorium, and we found the tickets in the costume of the Ghost of Christmas Present.

We took a break from our successful excursion to enjoy some of the holiday snacks. I chose a classic caramel popcorn while he went for a peppermint bark in the shape of a Christmas tree. We both chased down our food with hot cocoas topped with whipped cream and sprinkles and candy canes.

Really, it was the most fun I'd had in a long time.

"Hey!" Patrick yelled as we were strolling through some of the pop-up shops set up in the park. He pointed past the fountain to a little field that would be full of wildflowers come springtime. "The snowman building competition. We have to do that!"

He grabbed my hand and ran off to sign us up. I laughed as he dragged me along. I was finally blessed to have someone who loved Christmas as much as I did. It was always special to share these kinds of things with my friends and family too, but this was special in a new and exciting way.

"Okay, so what's our game plan, Oh Powerful and Magical Professional at Fun?" I asked him.

"I'm thinking big," he said, spreading his hands over the air like he was displaying something magnificent.

"Big?" I said flatly. "That's all you got?"

He shrugged. Then after a moment he said, "Maybe it's too on the nose, but what about Frosty the Snowman?"

I chuckled. "Oh, so now you're wanting to follow the rules. I thought you were going to say rabbit or turtle dove."

"Twelve days of Christmas!" he yelled excitedly.

"Only if we want to be disqualified for not having an actual snowman," I said, looking him right in the eye.

His gaze lingered on mine for a bit too long, making me forget that we were supposed to be in game mode. His excitement was infectious, but when he looked at me like that, I couldn't help but lose all ability to think or even move.

He pressed his forehead to mine, and for a moment I thought he was going to kiss me. I wasn't ready for it, so I froze. But he just wrinkled his nose and said, "Thanks for keeping me between the lines," he said.

Then he pulled away and trotted off to find snowman parts. When he came back he had helpers with him. He'd managed to attract the attention of a few kids who were interested in forming a team. I couldn't say no to them, and as much as I loved working with the kids, I also loved watching Patrick have fun with them and make them laugh.

We did a pretty fantastic job making a near-perfect replica of the classic animated Frosty the Snowman. It was actually hard rounding out his circular midsection and carving his fingers. Patrick had found the best hat and pipe he could, and we fastened on the eyes and nose, too. He carved out a smile, and while it looked exactly like the movie, it was a little simple. So we decided to add a bit of flair. For nearly an hour, the two of us carved out little scenes from the movie all over the body of the snowman. Patrick held up his phone while I drew the pictures with my fingers and with sticks and pine needles.

When we were satisfied with our work, we left to take a break. It would be another couple of hours before the judging would be finished. The kids ran off and started a snowball fight.

"What do you want to do next?" Patrick asked. "Sorry I pulled you into that one." He jutted his finger back at the snowman building contest behind us.

"It was fun," I said.

Patrick grabbed my hand and asked again. "I'm glad. But we're gonna do this right," he said. "I picked something, so now you pick something. What do you want to do? What would you hate to leave here having not done?"

I took pleasure in holding Patrick's hand. Between carving in the snow and just being outside in the cool air for so long, it was nice to have someone to warm up with. I glanced around the park and tried to imagine the map of the festival in my head. I really didn't want to do anything else that required being separated from Patrick. I wanted to hold his hand a bit longer. And there was something perfect I had in mind.

"Let's go!" I said. This time, it was my turn to drag him off. He trotted along behind me as I led him to the ice skating setup.

We were both a little breathless, and I could feel the cold nipping at my nose. Patrick's cheeks and the tips of his ears were red too. I stood up on my tip toes and resituated his beanie. He smiled at me with a look I hadn't seen from him yet.

"What is it?" I asked, suddenly growing excited with curiosity.

He wiped a few strands of fair from my forehead and tucked them safely behind my ear. "It's about time for me to get your scarf back to you," he said. But it felt like he was saying more than that.

We paid for our rental skates, and Patrick helped me to tie mine. Of course, I could have done it by myself, but I felt I had been too independent for too long. It was okay for me to find joy in letting him do simple things for me just because he wanted to. We stood, and I was the one to help Patrick stay steady and we entered the ring hand in hand.

For about thirty minutes, we skated around. Even when we both got our feet under us and built up our confidence, we chose to remain hand in hand and take it easy around the ring. Other people zoomed by us, and one couple put on a little figure skating show to *The Nutcracker* music. But Patrick and I took our time. We weren't in any kind of hurry.

After the skating, we sat down by the tree we'd helped to decorate and listened to some carolers. I convinced Patrick to join in just so I could hear his lovely voice again. Of course, he also made me sing along, but I didn't mind. It was fun, and it was something I loved to do.

Finally, it was time for us to check the results of the snowman building competition. We hurried over to the field and found that our snowman had a first place plaque placed on the ground in front of him.

"We did it!" Patrick said. "We got first place!"

He picked me up and spun me around in circles. Again, I thought it might be time for him to kiss me, but he didn't do it. Any other day I might have been let down by this, but we were having too much fun to get caught up on things like that. The kids eventually showed up, and we snapped a picture together with them and our snowman.

I got a copy and showed it to Patrick. "We look pretty good together, do you think?" he asked with a wink.

I nodded. "We certainly do."

Finally, it was time for dinner. There were food trucks and a big Christmas buffet with traditional food in the community center. We had a nice dinner, and after, when it was dark, we took another stroll around the neighborhood admiring the lights.

It felt like that one night when we'd almost kissed and the kids had interrupted us. I wondered about it the whole time we were walking in silence.

Then I saw it up ahead in a little garland-covered gazebo. There were several mistletoes hanging from the ceiling of it and a couple standing in the center, sharing a sweet kiss. My stomach flittered with the memory of the Santa Claus Ball. I wondered what the velvet-suited mystery man was up to right now. I glanced up at Patrick, who seemed totally serene. I wondered where his mystery woman was too. I'd heard Emily say that she saw him kiss someone that night. It made me a bit jealous to think about, but then again, I'd kissed someone too. And for a while, I'd thought that that was the most magical moment I'd ever shared with someone.

Part of me hoped that it was Patrick, but that would have been too perfect, and I knew life wasn't like that. All of the supposed magic I'd felt that night was probably just a result of my imagination and adrenaline. But this—I stared intently at Patrick until he looked back at me and smiled—this was real.

We walked a little farther hand in hand until the night wound down and my feet began to hurt. Patrick gave me a piggyback ride to his truck and then he drove me home, cranking up the truck's heater until I was almost sweating.

He walked me to the door and came up the steps with me. "I had a really great day with you," he said, taking my hands out of my pockets and interlacing his fingers with mine. "I'm glad I found you."

My tummy jumped and twirled. *This was it, right?*

I smiled and took a step closer to him. "Me too," I said.

"Can I see you tomorrow?" he asked.

I nodded. "I'd love that."

He gave a small smile and tightened his fingers around mine. Then, in a quick second, he leaned in and kissed me... on the forehead.

His lips were warm, and it still brought heat to my face, but I couldn't deny that I was a little let down. I bit my lip nervously, hoping that I didn't seem too dejected. After everything, the last thing I wanted to do was rush him into anything.

So instead, I buried my face into his shoulder like a shy woman. I fit perfectly there, and it was so natural and comfortable. It was like I'd been there before.

"Tomorrow?" he said, gently pulling away from me.

I nodded again. "I hope so."

He winked as he backed down the stairs. "I'll be here. And I'll have something for you."

He gave Carol, who had run out on the porch, a pat on the head and made me go inside before he drove away, but I watched him from the window as his taillights disappeared into the night.

CHAPTER 24

Patrick

MISTLETOE MOUNTAIN'S Christmas Eve party never seemed special before. I hadn't actually been to it since my parents died. Before that, I was young and I generally had fun, but I didn't fully appreciate it until I went with Holly.

When I was dating Emily, she always insisted that I use Christmas Eve as a vacation day. She didn't work, of course, and I always ended up just following her around shopping or whatever she felt like doing. I would see pictures that friends shared on social media and I would be interested in going. But even when I asked Emily if we could go, she would just say that she already made plans for us out of town or something.

With some distance from her now, I was actually free to do what I wanted. And I'd found someone I shared common interests with, someone I had fun with, someone I could confide in. She was someone... magical. And I didn't intend to let her think otherwise ever again.

Honestly, it was more than magical that I'd found Holly. It was a perfectly timed miracle.

I knocked on her door at nine in the morning. She'd agreed to meet me today, but I hadn't told her what time. I didn't really have a plan for the day other than to spend it with her, and I wanted to get an early start.

It took a couple of minutes for someone to reach the door. It opened slowly, and before me stood Holly's friend.

"Good morning!" I said cheerily. "It's Abigail, right?"

She blinked at me. "You're not going to do this all the time, right?" she said.

I chuckled. "It's a special day. I was excited."

A little smile twitched at the corner of her mouth. "Oh, Holly!" she sang over her shoulder. "You have a visitor!" She waved me to step inside the house.

Suddenly I was worried. "She is awake, right?"

Right about then, Holly came around the corner. She was dressed in a pair of powder blue sweats with little embroidered snowflakes on them. Her blonde hair was tied in a messy braid. Her eyes were heavy with sleep, and little bits of makeup were smudged under her eyes.

She stumbled into the living area where I was waiting. When her eyes locked onto me, she froze. She looked at Abigail, who was standing next to me with a smirk on her face, then she looked back at me. Without saying anything, she turned around and ran back to what I was assuming was her room.

"Huh," Abigail said. "I guess she didn't want to see you."

I knew she was joking, but I did feel a little bit bad about showing up suddenly. "Do you think it's okay if I go back there?" I asked. "Not inside… I'll just talk through the door, I guess?"

Abigail chuckled. "Yeah, she'd like to know she didn't scare you away."

I scanned the living area as I walked through. This was my first time being inside of Holly's house. It was just as I'd expected, full of Christmas. She and Abigail had a nice Christmas tree in the corner next to the TV, and underneath were several well-wrapped presents. I had seen the garland wrapping the porch and the lights on the outside of the house, so I knew they were decorators. Most people in town were, and considering Holly's love for Christmas, I had to assume she was too. There was the tree, some throw blankets and pillows, several little figurines here and there, and garlands around the house. It was cozy and cute, but not overdone.

"It's the room at the end," Abigail said from behind me.

I nodded. "Thanks."

As I approached Holly's door, I could hear her rustling around and muttering under her breath. I tapped on the door.

"One minute!" she yelled.

"Holly," I said through the door.

Then suddenly there was a little bark. Right, it must have been that cute little terrier I'd petted the other day. Carol, she'd said her name was. Carol was probably surprised to hear a stranger's voice right at the bedroom door.

"I already saw you," I said through the door. "And I still think you're beautiful, so open up."

The rustling quietened and I heard her footsteps slowly shuffling toward the door. She cracked it open, peering through with one eye. "That was very rude of you," she said. "It's too early for you to see me when I haven't had time to make myself look nice."

I noted the little black nose at the bottom of the door trying to push through and sniff me.

"I'm sorry," I said, taking a step closer to the door. "I just wanted to see you as soon as possible. I wanted to spend the whole day with you."

She sighed and opened the door the rest of the way. "Fine," she said. "I guess you'll get to see the whole mess–me and the room."

I grinned widely. She'd cleaned up her leftover makeup and was now barefaced. I could see her little freckles on her nose more clearly. She had a few red spots and lines under her tired eyes like any normal person would, and I drank in this natural sight of her. She had taken down her hair, and it fell in messy waves over her shoulder.

"I knew it," I said. "You're more beautiful than I remembered."

Holly rolled her eyes and flopped down on the edge of her bed. It was unmade, and I wondered if I had woken her up or if she never made it. There was a small stack of books on the nightstand. I wondered if she had read them all or if they were her stack to be read. She had a little desk by the window with pencils and markers strewn across it and an open planner with bright pictures and scribbles. Her closet was open, and a few items of clothing were lying haphazardly on the floor. I wondered if she was thinking about wearing them and decided not to or if they were dirty. Her dresser had a few items scattered across the top of it, a couple of necklaces and earrings, and a brooch.

There was a lot about her that I wanted to know.

"You should really give a girl a few minutes' heads up," she said.

I laughed and nodded. "Okay. This is the only time I'll surprise you—maybe."

I bent down and patted the little dog on the head. "Carol, like a Christmas carol?" I hadn't thought of that before.

She nodded and patted her bed. I thought it was an invitation for me to sit down, but the dog jumped up into the spot and laid down. I laughed at myself.

"So did you have a plan, or are you bombarding me just for fun?" she asked, crossing her arms and giving me a cute, mean stare.

I kneeled down on the floor in front of her bed and rested my hand on her leg. "I'm just bombarding you," I said confidently. "Then we're going out for the day."

She gave in to a smile but swiped my hand away. "Then get out so I can get dressed," she said.

"As you command," I said with a bow. I exited her room and Carol trotted along after me. Abigail was waiting in the living room with an expectant stare.

"You're lucky," she said, "in a couple of months, she'll yell at you if you do that."

I grinned. "I'm looking forward to it."

As I waited for Holly to get ready, Abigail and I talked. She had a unique sense of humor, but I liked her. She asked me about my friend

Andrew, but I couldn't tell if she was interested in him or if she despised him. I remembered that night we volunteered that there was something happening between them, but I couldn't figure it out. Maybe it was some strange attraction. Maybe they were natural enemies. But I made a note to get us all together soon so we could all figure it out.

Finally, Holly was done getting dressed. She came out wearing a deep red sweater and jeans and a pair of black winter boots. She'd left her hair wavy and a little wild, which I liked. But she'd put on makeup. Whatever she did was subtle, but her green eyes popped and caught my attention.

"Breakfast?" I asked her.

She narrowed her eyes at me. "You're supposed to tell me I look beautiful first," she said teasingly.

I laughed. "But I already told you that before you got dressed."

Abigail took a sip from her coffee mug. "Men. You know there's never a time you shouldn't tell your girlfriend that she's beautiful."

Holly took on an embarrassed sort of pink hue in her cheeks. She tucked her hair behind her bangs. "Oh, we're not... We haven't–"

I walked over to her and tucked her hair behind her ear on the other side. "You look beautiful," I told her.

She got flustered and even more red before doing that thing where she hid her face in my shoulder. I loved it when she did that.

Holly and I spent the day doing whatever we could think of. We ate a late breakfast then did some last-minute Christmas shopping. She helped me pick a gift for my aunt, and I kept my eye out for a gift for her Holly. Maybe it was a bit too soon, but I wanted to find something special for her.

We watched the final showing of *A Christmas Carol* in the theater then took another walk through town. Walking side by side and hand in hand with Holly was quickly becoming one of my favorite things to do.

But there was one other thing I was really looking forward to. I gave her scarf back to her like I'd intended to, but in light of recent events, I'd altered my plan slightly.

"About this Christmas Eve party," I said as we walked. "Have you ever gone?"

Holly nodded her head. "I went once a couple of years ago, but last year I didn't do much since I was gone for college."

"Did you go with someone?" I asked, curious if she'd had a man in her life at the time.

She just chuckled. "Yes. Abigail and Gretchen and Gretchen's boyfriend."

"Oh," I said, feeling a little relieved.

"Do you want to go?" Holly asked, looking up at me with her bright eyes.

It was funny. Emily would have never asked. She would have never assumed I wanted anything. Holly was so drastically different from her.

"I want to go with you," I told her.

She smiled. "Then let's go. I'd like to go with you, too."

It was so easy, so perfect. My chest filled with warmth.

HOLLY and I parted ways temporarily so we could get ready for the Christmas Eve party. It was a fancy function where people wore their best suits and dresses. The whole evening was a bit more elegant than the Santa Claus Ball. For starters, not everyone was dressed as Mr. and Mrs. Claus. You could actually see everyone's face.

I was always surprised that Emily didn't want to come to this kind of thing. It seemed like the perfect place for her to flaunt her parents' wealth and her expensive clothes.

I shook the thoughts of Emily from my head and walked arm in arm with Holly. She deserved my full attention, and I didn't want to get hung up on the past that had been haunting me for far too long.

I helped Holly take her coat off at the entrance. This was the first time I saw her in her dress without the hindrance of the coat. It was a long, silky navy blue color with thin straps and a slit up the leg. The dress itself was elegant and simple, but Holly looked ravishing.

"Pardon me for being redundant," I said in a mock British accent. "But you look quite beautiful, my lady."

Holly laughed. "You look rather dashing, too, my good sir," she said back in a surprisingly believable British accent.

We found our rhythm in the midst of all of the other people. It was a long, fun night of dancing and listening to the mini orchestra. There were trays of appetizers passed around and bubbly drinks served alongside them.

But there was one specific dance that I was waiting for... and it was almost time.

"I know Christmas isn't over yet," I said to Holly while we were seated. "But what has been your favorite part of this season so far?"

She leaned her shoulder into me. "Easy—meeting you."

I wrapped my arm around her shoulders. I was hoping that she would say that. "Are you sure? I caused you a lot of trouble there for a minute."

Holly glanced up at me from her eyelashes. "Aren't you worth the trouble?"

My heart skipped a beat, or more like stumbled through it. "I'll do my best to be."

"Then take the compliment," she said, laying her head on my shoulder.

We listened to the music and talked for a few more minutes until it was time. A lady announced over the speaker that the Christmas Darlings Dance was next. It was a special dance for couples. And while Abigail had nearly broken the ice for me, I wanted to tell Holly myself how I felt about her.

As the music started slowly, I took Holly's hand. "Will you dance with me?" I asked.

She nodded and squeezed my fingers. "I would love to."

My heart was pounding, not erratically, but solidly. I had found my confidence in her.

We swayed to the rhythm of the music. This was already so different from the Mistletoe Match. That dance was fueled by excitement and mystery and uncertainty. But I wasn't feeling any of those things now. I was feeling calm and certain.

"This is different from the Santa Claus Ball, right?" I asked her.

She looked up at me, confused. "Yes." She hesitated slightly as she said it.

Maybe she didn't know who I was, but that was okay with me. Because deep inside, not just superficially, I was sure she did. And I knew her, too.

"I never asked you," I said, cupping my hand against her back, "but you were there, weren't you?"

She searched my eyes and nodded.

The song was nearing the end already. It was almost time.

"There's something about you," I told her, wrapping my arms tightly around her back like I did that night.

Holly relaxed a little bit into me and wrapped her arms around me. Maybe, just maybe....

Just then, as the song was coming to a close, hundreds of strings of mistletoe dropped down to hang above us. She glanced up at the green plants with bright red bows, and a new kind of sparkle glistened in her eye.

I gently tilted her chin toward me. "Have you ever shared a magical kiss with someone?" I whispered to her.

She blinked at me, her eyes filled with wonder. She moistened her lips and looked at mine. "Once," she said, lifting onto her toes and pressing her lips to mine.

Much like that night, a plume of fireworks went off in my body. It was like every working part of me short-circuited and exploded with electricity. I squeezed Holly closer to me, pressing deeper into our kiss.

"There you are," I said after our kiss broke. "You were right under my nose the whole time."

Holly stroked my face with her hand. "I can't believe it was you. I thought it was too good to be true."

I smiled and kissed her once more for good measure.

CHAPTER 25

Holly

I couldn't have asked for a more perfect Christmas. Usually, it was just me and my parents out at their house making cookies and watching Christmas movies. But this year, we had a couple of extra people to celebrate with.

Early that morning, Patrick picked me up at home. This time, he gave me a twenty minute warning for his arrival so I had plenty of time to get dressed. It helped that I was already awake anyway. The excitement and anticipation of the day woke me up with the sun, so I had all of the time in the world.

I ran out to his truck as soon as he pulled in the driveway, not even giving him the chance to be a gentleman and come to the door. He got out anyway and greeted me with a warm kiss that made my heart flutter. He opened the passenger side door for me and picked up Carol to put her in my lap.

"You're ready early," Patrick said.

I shrugged nonchalantly. "You know. It's just my favorite day of the year and all, so I'm not really excited or anything."

He laughed and pulled us out of his driveway. We drove out of town to meet his aunt. I was so nervous to meet her. I'd never had to meet a boyfriend's parents before, so I wasn't sure what the protocol was. But Louise was sweet and greeted me warmly with a handshake. I'd almost expected her to be a hugger.

"Thank you for having us out," I said to her.

She waved her hand. "I'm happy to have you here," she said. "I needed to meet this girlfriend my nephew's been going on about anyway."

I peeked over at him and he scratched the back of his head. *How long had he called me his girlfriend to his aunt?*

We enjoyed a chat getting to know each other and then Patrick asked her how her project was going.

"What's your project?" I asked.

"Oh, Holly, you're going to love it!" Patrick said, jumping up. "" Let's show her!"

Louise pressed herself out of her chair. I took the moment to admire her strong arms and the confident, calm demeanor with which she moved. It reminded me of Patrick. I wondered how much of him was his aunt, how much was his mother and father, and how much was the part of himself he was finding after his time with Emily. I was excited to find out and learn more about him over time.

Louise led us to the garage, which was apparently her little wood-working workshop. She had a few unfinished projects here and there and lots of tools laying around. It was a bit disorganized, but it seemed like she had her own form of organization.

In the middle of the room was something big covered by a creamy canvas sheet.

"You ready for the big reveal?" Patrick asked excitedly. He looked more pumped up for this than Louise did.

"It's not finished yet," she said to me. "So it doesn't quite have the wow factor."

Before Patrick could say anything else and before I could tell her I was sure it was amazing anyway, she yanked off the canvas sheet and revealed a magnificent, huge sleigh. It was indeed unfinished, with only half of the carvings along the side completed. There were still rough edges that had yet to be sanded down. But I could tell that it was going to be so beautiful.

"Wow, this is amazing!" I said, going up and running my fingers along the rough etchings. It had a Nordic design, much like the one on display at the Santa Claus Ball. "I can't believe you're making a sleigh with your own hands!"

Louise effortlessly shouldered my praise. She seemed to know that it was amazing, but she wasn't bragging. We admired the sleigh, and Louise talked about her plans for finishing it. I told her I was excited to see the finished project and she promised that I'd be the first.

"Excuse me," Patrick said with feigned disbelief. "What about me? I'm your best friend and your nephew...."

Louise shrugged. "What can you say? I'm a girls' girl."

We went back into the house and chatted a bit longer. Louise got out some old photo albums and showed me pictures of their family. Patrick told me the stories behind a lot of them. I noted how he looked a lot like his mom, but he was built like his father with the same light brown hair.

"Oh! This picture is from our last Christmas together," Patrick said. He pointed into the photo album at a picture of his mom, her shirt covered with flour and a big smudge of icing across her face. She looked angry and was holding up a pair of oven mitts like she was about to hit someone. In front of her was a seventeen-year-old Patrick, laughing and arms braced in front of him. He, too, was wearing a coating of flour on his head and his hands were seemingly dipped in icing or batter. Behind him, his father was holding onto Patrick's shoulders, using him as a human shield to protect himself from his wife's attacks. He wore a mischievous looking grin, much like the one I'd seen on Patrick's face a time or two, and he was the only clean one in the picture.

They looked so happy together. And it broke my heart that they had been taken from Patrick too soon. I sniffled, and my eyes blurred with tears.

Patrick stroked my hair and pulled me into his shoulder to hug me. He didn't say anything, he just let me mourn for his family and for his lost youth. Even Louise gave me a pat on the back before leaving the room to fetch me a tissue.

I felt a bit ridiculous. This wasn't my family. If anyone was supposed to be crying, it was Patrick. But he stayed strong. When I finally glanced up at him, his eyes were tinged with red, but he wasn't crying. He kissed me on the forehead and didn't say anything.

After a while, it was time to head to my parents' house. Louise was going to pick up Mrs. Henson, so she was going to meet us there in her own vehicle.

I was excited for Patrick to meet my parents and see how they got along.

On the drive out into the country outside of Noel, Patrick and I listened to some Christmas music. We sang together. Carol curled up in the middle of the seat and rested her head on Patrick's leg. It was so precious, I couldn't even be jealous.

"I have something in store for you," I told Patrick as we pulled into my parents' driveway.

"Oh yeah?" Patrick asked, leaning over.

His eyes were begging for a kiss, so I planted a quick one on his lips. I caught him by surprise and his neck and ears flushed red. "That wasn't it," I teased him.

We got out of his truck and I let Carol go so she could run around in the snow freely. She tore through the drifts, bounding through them like a snow hare. She zoomed around the trees and decorations in the front yard, almost taking out baby Jesus in the nativity scene. We laughed and enjoyed watching her for a few minutes until Louise and Mrs. Henson pulled in behind us and got out of the car. I was surprised to find that they both looked a little nervous. But I couldn't blame them. It was somewhere new, after all.

I saw my parents rushing to the door through the big picture window. They swung open the door and rushed out to hug me. "Merry Christmas, cookie!" she said.

I was a little embarrassed by the nickname, but that was just my mother. My father pulled me in and gave me a kiss on the hair. "Please introduce us to your friends," he said, eyeballing Patrick.

I stepped back to give them a better view of Patrick. "This is Patrick," I said. And I turned to introduce Louise and Mrs. Henson, too.

My mom squinted at him. "You're that young handsome fella that came into the bakery, right?"

A light seemed to flick on in Patrick's head. "Yes! I thought you looked familiar! So you're Holly's parents?"

I looked at him, confused, but I decided to ask questions later.

My mom beamed and reached out to shake Patrick's hand. "Yes, yes! Now come in out of the cold."

My father held the door open for us as we filed into the house. It was warm and smelled like Christmas dinner–turkey and stuffing and some kind of pie.

"That must mean *you're* the van driver," he muttered into my ear.

I wasn't totally sure what he meant, but I didn't pay it any mind.

"We're looking at an early dinner, so I hope you all are hungry!" my mother said. "It'll be done in another hour."

"Perfect!" I said. "That gives us time for presents!"

"Have you still not grown out of that?" my dad teased, sinking down into the couch. "Ever since you were a little girl...."

I stuck my tongue out at him playfully.

"Let's chat first," my mom said, coming in and sitting next to my father.

So I indulged them. Even though I was excited to hurry up and open presents so I could give Patrick his, I did agree that it was best to get to know each other for a little while first. The conversation flowed naturally, seeing as my father was an excellent conversationalist and he could get anyone to talk to him about anything. Patrick talked a little bit about his family. Louise shared some of her stories about things she had created over the years, and Mrs. Henson talked about their friendship and how Patrick always came to help her. I was touched by how sweet he was, but then, that was Patrick.

Then it was time for our early dinner. We ate at around four o'clock, which seemed to happen every year. Maybe my mom planned it behind everyone's backs so we'd have time in the evening to get hungry and eat leftovers or make cookies for ourselves. I had missed making cookies in my parents' house, so I hoped that we would get to do it later.

We all tore through the dinner and stuffed ourselves. While we were waiting for our stomachs to ease, my father played some old videos of me opening presents on Christmas morning or me singing during the Christmas choir concert. Patrick and I sat close together on the couch, and he kept whispering in my ear how adorable I was.

Finally, I got my wish and we shared presents. Carol settled in next to the fireplace while we all took turns opening gifts. My parents had thoughtfully gotten Patrick a Christmas sweater and box of their famous gingerbread cookies. They'd given boxes to Louise and Mrs. Henson too, along with some nice-smelling candles. They both expressed that they were sorry they didn't bring anything because they hadn't expected to exchange gifts, but we all assured them that all we needed was their company.

I gave my parents their gifts first, then Louise and Mrs. Henson. Patrick had helped me choose things for them. I was glad Mrs. Henson had come. From what Patrick had said, she'd been feeling lonely since her husband had passed away.

I was surprised that Patrick had brought something for my parents, but I was grateful. He'd actually given them the tickets we'd won during the scavenger hunt, along with a beautiful set of antique golden ornaments.

And then he gave me a small box. It was wrapped in a nice glittery silver paper with curled ribbons around it. I eagerly slipped the ribbons off and tore open the paper.

"Oh, so you're that kind of present opener," Patrick muttered with a laugh.

I ignored his silly comment and opened the lid of the box. It was a beautiful, dainty necklace with a diamond covered holly. It was perfect.

"Wow. This is so beautiful," I said, feeling touched and also a little guilty for opening such a precious gift like a maniac.

Patrick smiled at me.

My mom smacked her lips and looked over at my father. "When we shared our first Christmas as boyfriend and girlfriend, you got me a pair of socks!"

Everyone in the room burst out laughing. "Well, we're not exactly...." I hesitated to confirm or deny the status of Patrick's and my relationship. I was pretty sure we were on the same page, but officially speaking, I didn't know.

I cleared my throat and patted Patrick on the leg. "Your gift is outside," I told him.

He looked puzzled, so I stood and pulled him to his feet. Everyone followed suit as we got on our coats and gloves and went out to the backyard.

There in the center of the yard were a couple of sleds. I didn't bother to wrap them up, but I had my parents place a big bow on each of them.

Patrick's mouth hung open. "You didn't...."

"I did!" I said giddily. "Wanna race?"

I took off first toward the sleds, but Patrick still beat me to them. We grabbed them and ran up the small hill. I was already exhausted but too excited to slow down by the time we got to the top.

"How do we start?" I asked him.

He wiggled his eyebrows at me. "You just go!" he said, taking a couple of giant steps and flinging himself down the side of the hill. I was surprised that he'd gone for it so quickly. I tried to match him, but I didn't start off right. When I landed on the sled, I was off-center. I didn't get very far before I tipped, and thankfully, I hadn't been going very fast. Patrick came rushing over, diving into the snow next to me.

"Are you okay?" he asked me, carefully touching my body.

I laughed. I hadn't had this much fun since... well, I didn't know when.

"I'm okay," I said, looking up at him. "I barely made it two feet. It's not like I took a big tumble." He looked worried at first, but then his face eased into a satisfied smile.

"Let's do this again next year," he said breathlessly, cupping my face and moving the hair that had found itself spread.

"You really want to?" I asked, my heart starting to thud in my chest.

He nodded. "You just have to promise me one thing."

I cocked my head to the side.

Patrick pressed his forehead to mine, the tips of our noses touching. "The next time someone calls me your boyfriend, you have to acknowledge it's true."

I chuckled. "I think I can manage that," I said, throwing my arms around him.

It was the best Christmas ever.

ALSO BY ID JOHNSON

Stand Alone Titles

<u>All I Want for Christmas is Pooch</u>

(*sweet contemporary romance*)

<u>Christmas Memory</u>

(*sweet contemporary romance*)

<u>The Doll Maker's Daughter at Christmas</u>

(*clean romance/historical*)

<u>Pretty Little Monster</u>

(*young adult/suspense*)

<u>The Journey to Normal: Our Family's Life with Autism</u> (*nonfiction*)

Silverwood Academy

(*paranormal romance*)

Vampire Hunter

World Builder

Realm Jumper

Celestial Springs

(*psychological thriller/literary fiction/women's fiction*)

<u>Beneath the Inconstant Moon</u>

<u>The First Mrs. Edwards</u>

<u>Leaving Ginny</u>

The Motherhood

(*dystopian romance*)

<u>Rain's Rebellion</u>

<u>Rain's Run</u>

<u>Rain's Return</u>

Ashes and Rose Petals

(contemporary romance/retelling of Romeo and Juliet and Cinderella)

<u>Girl in the Attic</u>

<u>Girl From the Tomb</u>

<u>Girl On the Beach</u>

Nashville Country Dreams

(contemporary romance)

<u>Meant to Marry Me</u>

<u>Lead Me Home</u>

<u>You Are the Reason</u>

Forever Love series

(clean romance/historical)

<u>Cordia's Will: A Civil War Story of Love and Loss</u>

<u>Cordia's Hope: A Story of Love on the Frontier</u>

The Clandestine Saga series

(paranormal romance)

<u>Transformation</u>

<u>Resurrection</u>

<u>Repercussion</u>

<u>Absolution</u>

<u>Illumination</u>

<u>Destruction</u>

<u>Annihilation</u>

<u>Obliteration</u>

<u>Termination</u>

A Vampire Hunter's Tale (based on The Clandestine Saga)

(paranormal/alternate history)

Aaron

Jamie

Elliott

Christian

The Chronicles of Cassidy (based on The Clandestine Saga)

(young adult paranormal)

So You Think Your Sister's a Vampire Hunter?

Who Wants to Be a Vampire Hunter?

How Not to Be a Vampire Hunter

My Life As a Teenage Vampire Hunter

Vampire Hunting Isn't for Morons

Vampires Bite and Other Life Lessons

Gone Guardian

Death Does Not Become Her

Blood of the Vampire Hunter (based on The Clandestine Saga)

(paranormal romance)

Night Slayer

Shadow Stalker

Queen Catcher

Mother Hunter

Father Finder

Ghosts of Southampton series

(historical romance)

Prelude

Titanic

Residuum

<u>Lusitania</u>

Heartwarming Holidays Sweet Romance series

(Christian/clean romance)

<u>Melody's Christmas</u>

<u>Christmas Cocoa</u>

<u>Winter Woods</u>

<u>Waiting On Love</u>

<u>Shamrock Hearts</u>

<u>A Blossoming Spring Romance</u>

<u>Firecracker!</u>

<u>Falling in Love</u>

<u>Thankful for You</u>

<u>Melody's Christmas Wedding</u>

<u>The New Year's Date</u>

Charles Town Brides (based on Heartwarming Holidays Sweet Romance)

(Christian/clean romance)

<u>From This Moment</u>

<u>Can't Help Falling in Love</u>

<u>It's Your Love</u>

<u>When You Say Nothing At All</u>

<u>My Girl</u>

<u>Unchained Melody</u>

<u>I Only Have Eyes For You</u>

Reaper's Hollow

(paranormal/urban fantasy)

<u>Ruin's Lot</u>

<u>Ruin's Promise</u>

Ruin's Legacy

When Kings Collide

(steamy historical romance)

Princess of Silence

Princess of Hearts

Collections

Ghosts of Southampton Books 0-2

Reaper's Hollow Books 1-3

The Clandestine Saga Books 1-3

The Chronicles of Cassidy Books 1-4

Celestial Springs Collection

Heartwarming Holidays Sweet Romance Books 1-3

Heartwarming Holidays Sweet Romance Books 4-7

Websites: https://books2read.com/ap/xX7ZD8/ID-Johnson

For updates, visit www.authoridjohnson.blogspot.com

Follow on Twitter @authoridjohnson

Find me on Facebook at www.facebook.com/IDJohnsonAuthor

Instagram: @authoridjohnson

Follow me on Bookbub: https://www.bookbub.com/authors/id-johnson

9 781964 125497